UNTIL NEXT TIME

RUBY DARE

For all those who love being fans. No matter what you are a fan of relish in your fandom and wave that fan flag high!!

~ BLOG SPOT ~
AND THAT'S ALL I HAVE TO SAY ABOUT THAT!

ALL THINGS EVERMORPH ALL THE TIME

SEASON 4

> **Episode Highlight:** Performance of Liam Caffney and Marnie Wethers.
> **Episode Lowlight:** Story continuity!!!

Alright you Everrites and Morphlings, Holy Hanna! The Fae are looking down upon this week's episode and are weeping! And not those good happy tears of "Yes! Preach our story!" but rather the sad angry tears of "What in the universal realms was that?!"

Okay, now to be fair there were some brilliant and masterful moments between Lochlan and Beatrice. The way Lochlan is trying to save even a small part of humanity and his blooming love for Beatrice that he is desperately trying to fight is coming through in the most beautiful inflections of the voice and subtle movements of his body. And you can see Beatrice fighting it as well. All her indecision is right there in her eyes! Almost had me in tears! Ah, but the rest of the show was truly cringe worthy.

Why you may ask? Well, let me tell you. But first let me ask you a question. Did the show get some new writers? Did they have a junior writer on staff they figured they would give a shot to? Listen, I'm all for giving a newbie a chance. We need to open the writing field. But, by the Goddess of Nyla put them on a very short leash! They MUST have some guidance, a senior writer to make sure they don't royally screw up! I watched no less than three instances where characters said the exact same lines as other characters from another season! VERBATIM! I kid you not!! What what? Come on! Continuity people! Let's keep some! Follow the story and be true to it! Do your research! If you need a script supervisor, I'm available. A keeper of history, a continuity nazi if you will, then I'm your gal! Call me! I'll come running (well, not running, because I hate running. But a speedy walk I'll give you)

And dear readers if you are scratching your head wondering what possible moments I could be talking about, well here you go. If you would be so kind as to look up these times on season 4 episode 8 - 15:12, 28:04, and 42:04 against season 2 episode 3 - 4:15,20:20 and 34:38. You too will be saying "Holy Fae-nal!"

Alright EverMorph Universe talk to me! Share your thoughts about my thoughts. What insights do you feel should be recognized from this episode? I want to hear it all!

Until next time EternallyEvers OUT!!

COMMENTS:

> Morphing4Oberon: Holy Hanna is right EterenallyEvers! I bet someone's head is rolling soon and not just because Rogan wants to start a war! Great catch!!

LochlanisMine: You did it again EE nice catch! You'd make a great script supervisor, although I'm sure some of the writers would disagree LOL

MorphlingsWillRise: Damn EE! Be nice! I'm sure some newbie is crying in his script as I type this!

NylaKingdom4Ever: EternallyEvers have you ever thought about writing a fanfic for EverMorphs? I think it would be fabulous!

I smiled as the comments on my blog started rolling. I loved that my followers started commenting almost immediately after I posted something. It was as satisfying as an eager student raising their hands when I asked a question. Smiling, I closed my laptop. Tomorrow was an early day, which meant tonight needed to be an early night.

My short heels clicked against the newly polished floors as I headed to my classroom. Tomorrow would be the first day back from Christmas break, and I wanted to rearrange the desks. No matter how many times I changed them around, the cleaning crew always put them back into standard formation when they were done cleaning.

This time I had waited until they had finished with my room before starting the change. My seniors would be starting a new section in the morning, and true to form I always did a new room configuration when a new section was beginning. This time it would be *Chaucer's Canterbury Tales.*

I flipped the lights on and put my bag down on the desk. I put my long black braids up in a bun and started moving desks into two octagons with a center space for me to teach from if I wanted to. I needed to make the center space a little large. As a plus size woman I made the world adjust to me, not the other way around. It had taken me some time, but I loved every inch of my mocha brown body. All the curves, lumps, bumps, and dimples equaled love. It was who I was, and I refused to apologize for it.

I was quick to cut people out of my life who tried to change me, well meaning or not. Those who tried to lead me down a path of what they believed would be a healthier, thinner, and therefore happier life for me, found themselves looking at my back and hips as I sashayed away from their lives.

Once the new room design was done, I pulled fresh folders out of my bag. One for every student. Inside held the syllabus for the new unit, a pack of blank college ruled paper, a list of resources that would help my students study and understand Chaucer better, and of course five self-designed stickers. It was my trademark.

Homemade stickers that exemplify the feelings my students may exhibit while diving into the material. This particular unit had WTF?!? coming out as steam from a cup of coffee, an exploding head with '*My head hurts*' coming out the top, and one with two cats walking in opposite directions but their tails were entwined and underneath it read Keep Calm and Read On. Next to last was a year calendar with a red circle around a date. Above it was the word Done!

The very last sticker in the collection never had to do with the unit of material. It was always a secret homage to my favorite television show *The EverMorphs*. It was two moons with the shadow of fairy wings behind the second moon. It was so subtle. So subtle that most of my students would think it was an eclipse because they knew I loved astronomy. What they didn't know is that it was an

insignia I had created to represent The House of Nyla.
They were the ruling family in *EverMorphs*.

It gave me a warm giggle to know I was secretly
sharing a small part of myself with my favorite humans. It
was a secret I kept close to the vest. Only my best friend,
Tess and of course my online community knew; with them
I openly shared my love of *The EverMorphs*, but even they
did not know my true identity, only my online persona. It
was safe and I could freely share so much of myself with
like minded people without ever worrying about reper-
cussions.

I had my reasons for keeping this part of myself a
secret. I had seen enough online videos and interviews
with celebrities talking about 'their fans'. I was an
observer, not only of words but of actions and movements.
Celebrities could verbalize how much they *loved* their fans
until the cows came home. But their body language gave
them away everytime. Their body ticks often betrayed
their proclamations of love. I could always pick up on it. It
was the one time actors were terrible at acting.

I nodded in satisfaction as I placed the last folder and
took a final look around the room. I grabbed my bag as I
flipped off the lights and headed for home. Tomorrow was
going to be an interesting day.

~ LIAM ~

I collapsed onto my couch as I took a deep calming breath. It had been a long day on set, but a good one. Only four more episodes needed to be filmed for the season. So that meant three, maybe four more months of shooting. Arlene, my agent, had sent over a pile of scripts that would fit into my off-season time and still leave several weeks of complete downtime before *Ever-Morphs* started filming season nine. We had already been renewed for seasons nine through twelve which was unheard of in hollywood. There had been a lot of chatter surrounding the announcement.

I looked at the pile, then decided I needed a snack before jumping into the fray. I stood, letting my long legs stretch as I headed to the kitchen. I put the water filled tea kettle on the stove, and then mixed several different types of tea leaves to make my own special blend of chai tea. While I waited for the kettle to boil, I whipped up a grilled cheese and tomato sandwich. With two types of cheese and thick bakery fresh whole wheat bread it was an indulgence. I tried to keep lean and trim when shooting, but if I had a craving I allowed myself to indulge. It was one of my rules. Life was too short not to indulge every now and then.

Sandwich and tea in hand I headed back to the living room. I made myself comfortable as I folded my legs underneath me. I put my long, dark curls back into somewhat of a bun. I enjoyed the long hair but I was looking forward to cutting it once filming was done. I couldn't cut it too short but I wanted it shorter than it was now. I took a bite of my sandwich and started flipping through the pile just looking at the titles.

I knew I would read all of them, but for now I was looking for a title that would grab my attention. As I came close to the bottom of the pile and finished off my sandwich, I stopped at a script entitled *Hidden Tales*. Maybe it was the font or just the implication that something was hidden deep within the tales. but whatever it was, I picked up the script and started reading it.

I pulled a blanket across my body as I got lost in the script. Time slipped passed as I read and then re-read the script. This was it, this was the show I wanted. It was a retelling of *The Canterbury Tales*. Modern with a little dark twist. I was intrigued with the part they were looking at me for, the pardoner.

I briefly remembered reading *The Canterbury Tales* in high school. I liked it then, but that was all I could really remember about the experience. I drained my tea and headed to the shower. It was late, so I decided to wait until tomorrow to call Arlene. *Hidden Tales* would be a nice change from *The EverMorphs*. I couldn't pass what would be a short commitment for something so new and interesting. I just needed to land the part.

The next morning I woke up, got ready for work and called my agent. "Hey Leenie, sorry, I know it's early, but I have to be on set soon. But I wanted you to know I'm really interested in *Hidden Tales*. So whatever needs to happen, let's do it."

I could hear Arlene clapping her hands in triumph. "Excellent! I was hoping you would pick that one. I'll get in touch with the producers today. Liam, before I let you go, how do you feel about attending a little fan event?"

I rolled my eyes. "Leenie, you know I love my fans but with my schedule, I just don't think—"

"No, no, this is a simple one. It's at an animal shelter. It's more about getting people to adopt than anything else. You'll be spending more time with animals than with fans. Only four hours next Saturday."

"Leenie—"

"Sign some autographs, take a few photos. I thought you loved your fans." Arlene teased.

"I am keenly aware that I am where I am in my career not just because of my talent, but because of my fans as well, it's just sometimes they are a little much." She always had a way of making me feel guilty. But I was going to put my foot down this time. Or at least try to. "Besides, will it even fit into my shooting schedule? We've been shooting quite a few weekends lately."

Arlene cleared her throat. That was never a good sign. "Don't get upset, but I already cleared it with the people at *TEM* yesterday. They were gracious enough to make a small change in the shooting schedule so I could whisk you away to Connecticut for two days without completely ruining the schedule or making them go over. Honestly, they were very accommodating. I have a feeling more than one of them has a rescue animal waiting for them at home."

I pinched the bridge of my nose and took a deep breath. I hated when she orchestrated shit like this behind my back! But she had been my agent and friend for many years. I should know better by now. *'Ask forgiveness, not permission.'* That was her motto. "Fine Leenie, I'll do it. I'll go to Connecticut in the middle of winter for you. Just email me the details."

I could hear Arlene smiling into the phone. "And this is why you're my favorite client, and it's practically Spring really."

"Ha! Spring my ass, it's barely the middle of January." I snorted. "I assumed I was your favorite because of the ten percent I keep putting in your pocket."

Arlene laughed. She knew I was kidding. "Tsk, tsk, it's too early to be so cynical. Now go to work and I'll email you about the event and *Hidden Tales*. Ciao for now." Arlene hung up.

I put my phone in my bag and headed for the door. Another long day was waiting for me on set.

~ ABIGAIL ~

I stepped out of the shower, and enveloped myself in a big fuzzy towel and then took my braids out of the bun they had been in. I continued my morning ritual as I listened to some classic rock on Pandora. Five songs later and I was out the door headed to Odyssey High School. Home of the fighting blue sharks.

I had my senior honors English class first period. Several of those students were also in the drama club, of which I was proudly the advisor. I knew those few would probably come up with the most elaborate presentations for the Chaucer section. I was already looking forward to seeing it. I hummed a tune as I walked into my classroom. I was pleased to see that the janitorial staff had not moved my fabulous figure eight.

As I was writing the first assignment on the board Margot came in. Margot was one of my favorite students. But I would deny having favorites if anyone asked. She was a chubby girl that in college would either solidify herself as a plus size beauty or slim down to a societal "average" woman. Either way, I hoped she would always be strong in the belief of who she was.

Margot was smiling as she handed me a printout. "Ms. Reese, did you see this? I think you should enter. You're a fan of the show, right?"

I took the printout from Margot and read it. *The Ever-Morphs* were running a nationwide contest for drama students. I sucked in my breath, as I mustered up a smile for Margot. "What would I need with a contest like this? And what exactly is an EverMore? Sounds like something from Edgar Allen Poe."

Margot took the paper back and laughed. "It's *Ever-Morphs*, Ms. Reese, but I have a sneaky suspicion that you knew that already."

I just stared at Margot, trying not to reveal anything.

"It's okay Ms. Reese, from one Everrite to another, your secret is safe with me." Margot gave me a Cheshire cat smile and a wink, then headed to her desk. She picked up the folder and immediately pulled out the stickers. "I love it when you make us new stickers!"

I relaxed a little. If there was anyone I could talk with about *EverMorphs* and have it kept a secret , it would be a person like Margot. But still, I needed to keep some things just for myself. "I'm glad you like them. Just remember that when you are rooting through the mind that is Chaucer."

The other students started filing in. I straightened my posture and smiled. "Welcome back from break. I hope you all had some fun and got some rest because we are about to delve into a world you have never been to before. Chaucer's *Canterbury Tales* is a challenge, as well as a delight for the mind."

Tanner raised his hand and began speaking. "Do we have to read it in its original form, or do we get to use a modern version?"

I pointed to the folder on his desk. "Take out the stickers in the folder and you tell me."

Tanner looked at the stickers and his shoulders slumped as he sighed. "Original form."

I stifled a laugh. "I'll try to make it as painless as possible. This is one of my favorites and hopefully by the time we are done, it will be a favorite of yours too." I started passing out the books. "Now let's dive in, shall we?

~ LIAM ~

The week had passed quickly and instead of relaxing at home in my jacuzzi, I was on a plane heading to a pet adoption fan event. I hoped it would be better than I expected. I smiled at the flight attendant as she handed me a drink before take off. I enjoyed the perks of first class. I took a sip, then put it down as I picked up my copy of Chaucer's *Canterbury Tales*. The *powers that be* had liked my taped audition, but the deal for the role of the Pardoner wasn't set in stone yet. Still, I wanted to familiarize myself with the original text the show was derived from.

I had bought a copy online with the original text without the handy modern version on the next page. I figured, why not fully commit? But on my third round of reading through the same paragraph in the Pardoner's Tale I began to regret my decision to not get the modern version.

I didn't have time to dwell on it because I felt a small hand lightly tap my shoulder. I turned to see a little girl with fairy ears on and an Everrite family crest necklace around her neck. She looked scared. She couldn't have been older than ten. I smiled, trying to put her at ease.

"Well hello there. And what might your name be?"

"My, hi, my name is, are you Lochlan?"

I did my best to turn my smirk into a smile. I hated when *fans* couldn't separate the actor from the character. But she was a little girl. Little children were the exception to all my fan rules. Well, the nice ones anyway. I turned to the little girl. "Why yes, I am. And who might you be, my little fairy?"

The little girl giggled. "My name is Stella. You're my favorite!"

"Aren't you the sweetest?" I looked around for a lurking parent poised with a phone taping our interaction. I didn't see any. I leaned in close to Stella. "Don't tell Isla, but *you,* Miss Stella, are *my* favorite fairy."

Stella giggled. "Can I please take a picture with you? I need proof, or my friends won't believe me."

I ran my fingers through my hair, trying to make it look decent and get rid of the hat head. I unbuckled my seat belt and sat up a little straighter. "Of course darlin' Anything for my favorite fairy."

Stella fumbled with her phone for a moment. She was so nervous.

"Here Stella, let me take the pic. Longer arms and all." I wrapped my free arm around Stella, sticking my other arm out into the aisle to get us both in the shot. "Say "Long live Nyla!"

"Long live Nyla!" Stella smiled.

I took two pictures and handed the phone back to Stella. Just then her mother came running up the aisle.

"Stella! I told you not to bother him!" She turned to me. "I am so sorry. I hope she wasn't too much of a bother."

I gave Stella's mom a million dollar smile. She seemed a little too uptight. Stella really hadn't bothered me. She was a very sweet girl. "No trouble at all. It's always nice to meet another fairy from the realm." I winked at Stella.

"Well, we'll let you enjoy the rest of your flight in peace. Won't we, Stella?" The mother gave Stella a little pinch on the arm.

"Sorry to bother you, Lochlan." Stella looked down at the floor.

I hated parents like this. Especially when the child was so nice. I took Stella's hand and gave it a kiss. "No need to apologize, it was my greatest pleasure to have met you."

The mother gave Stella a gentle shove to make her go back to her seat. She looked back at me and waved, then headed back down the aisle. The mother watched her go. "Again, sorry for the trouble."

I tipped my glass at her and smiled. Once the mother was gone, I went back to reading. I sighed in frustration, It was taking me longer than I expected to truly digest the reading. If I got the role, I would think about getting a tutor, depending on how close the show stayed to the source material. My interest in Chaucer had been rekindled with the possibility of this role. I closed the book, leaning back against the chair and closing my eyes for the rest of the flight.

I was startled when I saw Arlene waiting for me in baggage claim. "There he is! My number one client. How was the flight?" She gave me a hug and kiss.

"Leenie, what a nice surprise! I wasn't expecting you." She really was a great friend.

"Well, since I kind of strong-armed you into doing this, I figured I'd better show up and give you some support."

"Ah, you really are a doll. Thanks for coming. I'm ready to face the masses!" I grabbed my bag and hers.

"Slow down there, cowboy. First I'm taking you to dinner. The masses will happen bright and early tomorrow." Arlene looped her arm through mine. "Come on, let's get you to the hotel and all checked in."

~ BLOG SPOT ~

AND THAT'S ALL I HAVE TO SAY ABOUT THAT!

ALL THINGS EVERMORPH ALL THE TIME

MID EPISODE DEVELOPMENT ALERT!!

Greetings my favorite fairies. I know it's not my usual blog day, but a little butterfly floated something past me that I had to pass along to my realm. So here we go, I hope you are all sitting down. Our beloved NeverMorph is running a contest. And not just your run of the mill contest. That's good right? Well, you might not think that when I tell you more. Please stop me if you've heard this. Oh, wait you can't. So, if you know what I'm talking about just scroll down and leave a comment on who you think is behind the curtain spying on Lochlan and Beatrice under the moonlight. Which hopefully we will get the answer to on the next episode

Now, back to the contest. A proclamation has been called across the kingdom of Nyla. Apparently, the Queen along with her faithful and valiant (not to mention smoking hot) son, Lochlan, are holding a royal contest. To bequeath their glorious attendance at a performance. This contest is for high school drama teachers/coaches, so if you know any, sound the alarm and bring them into the fold of knowledge! The best royal request as to why the queen and her favorite son should help the drama clan of (insert school name here) will win. The winners will be granted a visit by the queen and her son in person! How does one enter the contest and in what form must the request be in? That is a very good question. The rules seem a bit vague but go to the EverMorphs official site to get the true blue lowdown.

Now, I have no idea why the show decided to do this. Who knows what the powers that be have going on in their minds. But it's an opportunity for a teacher and her students to be touched by the magic of EverMorphs for a brief time in the cosmos. So sound the trumpets and spread the word. Until the next episode...........

EternallyEvers OUT!

COMMENTS:

NylaKingdom4Ever: Thanks for the update EE! My best friend is a drama teacher. I'll be passing this along to her. EternallyEvers are you entering?

> EternallyEvers: What makes you think I teach drama ;)

BeatriceBabe: I think it's Isla spying on Lochlan and Beatrice. She is just so jellie!

RogansRaiders: I think it's one of Rogan's spies. He needs some dirt to get some leverage against Lochlan.

IdolofIsla: My students are already working on a presentation fit for royalty! What a great opportunity!!

LochlanisMine: Why only drama teachers?! No fair!!

MorphlingsWillRise: Sorry LochlanisMine, you win some you lose some. If it makes you feel any better, I can't enter either. I think it might be part of a larger campaign to keep the arts alive in the public school systems. There are a couple of other shows from the same streaming service doing similar things.

MorphingforOberon: It's gotta be Nyx. She's Isla's first maiden. You all know she thinks Lochlan is cheating on Isla with Beatrice. That little fairy is out for proof. Also, I think she is secretly in love with Isla so.....

BeatriceBebe: Yes! Nyx totally is in love with Isla! So if it's not Isla directly I can absolutely see Nyx venturing out on her own to learn the truth. I can't wait for the big reveal!

~ ABIGAIL ~

My alarm went off several times before I groaned and rolled over, slapping it to turn it off. I curled back over to catch some more zzz's before I truly had to get up. The sun peeking through the blinds had other ideas. I sighed as I rolled out of bed and down to the kitchen to make myself some cinnamon coffee. I looked out the window and smiled, it was the perfect day for a pet adoption fair. The sun was shining, and the forecast promised no snow and a comfortable temperature, a little above average for January.

Several years ago I had wanted to start doing some charity work in my community. I had volunteered at a local food bank, a senior community center and for the last three years I had been volunteering two Saturdays a month at **The Giggles and Cuddles Animal Shelter.** This Saturday was their annual big event. It was their push for not only adoptions but funds to keep the center going.

I looked down at my two treasures, Lochlan and Beatrice as they circled my legs. I gave them each a scratch, but they were mewing for their morning meal. I quickly made their breakfast, gave them a few more ear scratches, and headed up to my room to get ready for the day.

I loved the drive to the shelter. It was all back roads filled with open fields and trees. It was only twenty minutes, but it was a serene twenty minutes. I lived outside of New Haven, in one of Connecticut's smaller towns. It was a dramatic difference from the concrete of Manhattan, and that had been the main draw for me to accept the teaching position at Odyssey High. It was perfect, I had the greenery and nature I wanted but the small city of New Haven was just a hop, skip and a jump away. And Manhattan was only a short train ride away. It really was the perfect location for me. It made me sigh in contentment just thinking about it.

When I arrived at the shelter, everyone was running around trying to get things ready. Post holiday adoption drives were always the hardest. So many pets had been given as gifts for Christmas and Hanukkah and then brought to the shelter when it wasn't all fun and games for the new owners. It always frustrated me how people didn't understand the responsibility of a pet until it was too late and it was always the pet who suffered for it. That's why this event was so important and today I had a feeling it was going to go very well.

I found the manager to find out my assignment for the day. "Hey Steve, where do you need me?"

A look of relief came over his face. "Oh Abi! Thank god, you are here! I need you in the puppy pen today."

"Sure! No problem. Oh, are we doing the twenty-five dollar adoption special today?"

"Yes, but there is something more important you need to be doing while in the pen."

I cringed. "Oh no, Steve! You aren't sticking me with a newbie, are you?"

Steve gave me one of his best smiles. "Kind of, but not really. We have a celebrity here to help boost the adoptions and raise some funds. He'll be spending a good portion of his time here with the puppies because we have more than we can handle at the moment and really need to get some adopted today." Steve rushed his words, not giving himself a breath.

"Breathe, Steve! Alright, I guess. So tell me, who will I be babysitting today?"

Steve's whole body seemed to relax. "Oh thank you Abi, I knew I could count on you. I was so afraid to put him with one of the younger volunteers."

"Hey!" I laughed. I knew he wasn't calling me old. We were both in our early thirties. I just liked teasing him.

"Oh! Sorry, I meant that he's from a popular show and I was afraid younger ones wouldn't be able to control themselves. I know what a scholarly reader you are. I didn't think you would get all loopy around him."

I smiled. "Thanks? I guess. So tell me, who is this guy anyway?"

"His name is Liam Caffney? He's on a show called The EverPeople? No, no, *The EverMorphs*. Have you heard of it?"

I put all of my college acting techniques into action and kept a blank and even keeled look on my face. "I haven't watched it myself, but some of my students talk about it every now and then."

Steve nodded. "That's what I thought. It's more of a teen, early college age type show, right?"

I could have gone into an entire diatribe as to why that was a completely false and ignorant statement. Instead, I just nodded.

Steve handed me two shirts. "One for you and one for Liam, he should be here in about fifteen minutes."

I smiled. "Great! That gives me just enough time to change into my shirt and then I'll get the pen ready." I walked off to the bathroom.

Once inside the ladies' room, I checked the stalls to make sure I was alone. Assured of my solitude I did a little happy dance in the bathroom that lasted maybe fifteen seconds before reality crashed in. I was going to be in an enclosed space with one of my favorite actors who happened to play my favorite character on my favorite television show! He couldn't know I was a fan. I had to keep my cool. But how could I even look him in the eye without gushing over him? Or worse, be stone cold and say nothing? I splashed some water on my face, and looked in the mirror for a little chat with myself. "Hold it together Abi! You've got this. He's just some guy from a show you like. It's fine. Remember why you are here. It's all about the pups and kitties today," After all, if I could teach in front of a bunch of hormonal teenagers day after day I could do this.

I changed into my event shirt. Looking in the mirror one last time before leaving the bathroom, I wished I had put some lipstick on, maybe some eyeliner and mascara before leaving the house. I laughed at myself for acting like a giddy schoolgirl. Running some cold water over my hands I took several deep breaths to calm myself. I looked through my purse and found a lipstick that was subtle in color. It was what I considered a day shade and it would go well with the coral color in my shirt.

Now that I was composed, I was ready to get this event underway. I grabbed the shirt for Liam and stared at it for a moment. A smile wiggled its way across my face as an idea came to mind. I quickly went and found Steve.

He was in the lobby area. "Steve! I have an idea. These shirts, we have a bunch, right?"

Steve nodded. "We've got a couple of boxes full. Why? Do you need another one?"

"No, I mean yes. I mean we should ask this Liam guy to sign some, and then we can sell them. If he's as popular as you say, I bet they will sell out. Make more money for the shelter, right? Maybe twenty-five or thirty dollars a piece? Is that too much?"

Steve snorted. He looked around then put his arm around me. "Between you and me, I'm a huge science fiction fan. I haven't watched his show, but I've been to conventions where his show has had panels. Their merch is super expensive and sells out almost every time."

"So good! Let's do twenty- five for pre-signed and fifty for personalization? Wait, do you think he would do it?"

Steve smiled. "Only one way to find out. Here he comes now."

I turned as Liam and a woman approached us. I could feel myself getting dizzy. He had a dazzling smile and his longish hair was up in a bun with some loose curls spilling out. I put my hand in my pocket and pinched my thigh to bring myself back to reality.

Arlene put her hand out. "Hi, I'm Arlene, I was told you were Steven, the man with a plan."

Steve shook her hand. "Steve, please. Welcome to our little shelter."

Liam looked around. "I'd say more than little. This place looks amazing."

"Steve, this is Liam Caffney." Arlene introduced him.

Steve shook Liam's hand. "It's very nice to meet you. And this is my top volunteer, Abigail. She's going to be guiding you through your day here with us."

"Ah cheers! Good deal. It's nice to meet you, Abigail." I could see Liam give me the once over.

If I had to guess, he was checking my body language to see if I was a fan. I was a master at masking any fan vibe for any occasion. He couldn't sense anything from me. I could see it made him relax a bit.

"Abi here came up with an idea we hope you are game for."

Liam smiled. "Try me."

"First we have a shirt for you to wear today." I handed him his shirt.

"We actually have a lot of these shirts," Steve stated. "We were hoping you would be willing to sign some so we could use them to sell, and raise even more money for the shelter today."

"I think I can handle that." Liam nodded.

I looked at Steve and then back at Liam and Arlene. Apparently I needed to be the one to ask for the really big part. "We were also hoping you might be willing to do some personalizations on the shirts for a bit more money."

Arlene shook her head. "I don't know about that. He'll gladly sign a pile before we begin though."

Liam waved. "Hi, right here in the room. It's no problem, Leenie. If it raises more money, I say let's do it."

"Okay, but only for a limited time. Not the entire time he is here. Let's say an hour."

"Let's say two," Liam chimed in.

I was doing my best not to get too excited. And also resisting the urge to smack this Arlene character. She was a bit too controlling for my liking. "Are you sure? I know we threw this on you last minute," I gave Arlene a side glance. "It's perfectly fine to say no. Just you being here will raise more money than not."

"Oh, so you're a fan of the show?" Arlene asked.

I shook my head. "I'm afraid not. I'm more of a reader. But I have quite a few students who are big fans."

"She's an English teacher at the local high school," Steve chimed in.

I nodded. "I just started my honor seniors on Chaucer's *Canterbury Tales*."

Liam gave Arlene a look, then gave me one of his red carpet smiles. "Really? Then we certainly have a lot to discuss. I just started reading it again. Haven't picked it up since university, but recently I felt the urge."

I raised an eyebrow. Not many people got an *urge* to randomly pick up Chaucer. "Of course. We can discuss it as you sign some shirts."

Liam laughed. "Ah, a real taskmaster I see. Well, lead the way!"

"Um, shirts are in the storage room. Let me get them." Steve turned in the direction of the stock room.

"No worries, mate. I'm sure Abi here can lead the way. As long as there is a table, I can sign away from there." He looked at me. "You don't mind if I call you Abi, do you?"

"No, that's fine."

Liam put his arm out to me. "Shall we?"

Steve turned to Arlene. "Thank you again for this. We are really excited to have Liam here."

"It's our pleasure. I'm always happy to help my great uncle when he calls. This place was just a dream when I was a kid. It warms my heart to see how far his dream has come. And besides, Liam loves giving back to his fans, and he's a big animal lover, so it's perfect. Isn't that right Liam?"

"Absolutely, but I really should get to signing."

I looped my arm in Liam's and we started for the storage room.

"Stop by the office and get some sharpies first!" Steve yelled after us.

I put my thumb up in the air giving the okay sign.

"Let me show you where he and Abi will be stationed." I could hear Steve's footsteps as he led Arlene to the puppy pen in the front room.

~ ABIGAIL ~

I pulled out a chair and handed Liam a couple of sharpie markers. "I'll grab you some shirts." I went to different boxes making sure I pulled out shirts in all sizes, tossing them at Liam as I pulled. One of the other volunteers walked in looking for me.

"Hey Abi, do you know where the extra leashes—" Simone stopped mid-sentence. "Holy crap! You're Lochlan!"

Liam smiled but said nothing.

"Simone, this is Liam. Who is Lochlan?"

Liam stifled a laugh.

Simone pointed to Liam. "That's Lochlan, crown prince of Nyla in the realm of Everly. Oh my god! Can I have your autograph?!" Simone practically shrieked.

"Simone! Get a hold of yourself. We are not at a boy band concert!"

Liam laughed out loud. "Wow, I don't think I've ever been compared to a boy band before."

Simone's cheeks turned red. "Sorry. Um, I came in here for something."

"You mean something besides getting an autograph?" Liam winked at her. "Perhaps hoping to grab a photo?"

I rolled my eyes, but secretly I was tickled at how he was joking and razzing Simone. However, it was moments like this that showed why I would never let him or anyone else I worked with know I was a fan. He was nice enough, but he was treating her differently than he was treating me. It was subtle, but it was obvious enough to me, although Simone seemed clueless. "I believe you were looking for the extra leashes.

"Abi, if you grab those extra leashes, I'll take a quick picture here with - I'm sorry, what's your name?"

"Um, Simone. I'm Simone. Really? I can take a picture with you?"

Liam nodded. "I'll even sign your shirt if you want."

All Simone could do was nod her head and smile.

Liam got up and walked over to Simone and held out his hand. "It's very nice to meet you, Simone. Thank you for watching the show. I'm so glad you like it."

Simone just kept nodding. "It's my favorite show on the air. I never miss an episode. Will you end up with Beatrice or are you going to marry Isla?!"

"Sorry lass, I can't answer that question. But promise me you'll keep watching to find out."

"Of course!" Simone smiled. She pulled out her phone to take a picture, and promptly dropped it on the floor.

Liam picked up her phone. "Allow me, darlin'. Smile pretty." Liam took the picture then handed the phone back to Simone. "Now, about that shirt."

"You can sign my chest if you like." She stuck out her chest for Liam.

"Simone!" I admonished.

"I just meant the front!" Simone snapped back.

"How about I sign here on your sleeve?" Liam didn't wait for an answer, he signed the sleeve and went to sit back down.

I handed a box of leashes to Simone. "Here you go, better get them out there." I turned Simone towards the door and gave her a nudge to get moving. Once Simone was gone, I turned towards Liam. "Sorry about that, but I have a feeling you are used to it."

Liam shook his head. "I don't know if I'll ever get truly used to that. However, I am very thankful for my fans. Without them, I have no series."

"Understandable, I guess. There's a chance she won't be the last staff member to treat you like that today, no matter what Steve may tell them. I'll do my best to keep them at bay."

Liam shrugged. "It comes with the territory. Thank you though."

"Sounds like you don't enjoy that part of the job."

Liam shrugged again. "You have to take the good with the bad."

"So you consider your fans bad?"

I t took me a moment to realize what Abigail had just asked me. My eyes grew wide as I vehemently shook my head. What was I doing? How could this woman I just met put me so at ease to let my guard down? What if she repeated what I had said? It was easy enough to deny since only the two of us were in the room. I knew how to deal with tabloid bullshit. But I had to answer her. "Oh no! That's not what I meant at all. It's just complicated I guess."

Abigail knew she had put me on the spot. I could sense she wanted to let me off the hook. She smiled to put me at ease. "Well let's not complicate it for you today. Let's just get some pets adopted." Abigail playfully threw another pile of shirts at me "Follow me."

Abigail led me to the puppy pen. It was in a front room just off of the front doors. Steve had already set up the table and chairs for the two of us to sit at and for people to fill out adoption forms or get a shirt signed by me. The puppies clamored to the side of the pen with happy yaps aimed at me.

I chuckled at their cuteness. "They are adorable! Can I get in there with them?"

"Be my guest." Abigail laughed.

I climbed in and began to play with the puppies. I chuckled and smiled as they licked at my face and jumped on and off my lap like I was their own personal pride rock. It was glorious. This alone was worth coming. The puppies made me feel like we were off in our own little world, a world filled with puppy love. Out of the corner of my eye I could see Abigail watching me. There was pure joy on my face and I didn't try to hide it, and I didn't care who saw it. If I allowed myself to think about it I would have to admit that I needed more pure joy in my life. I needed to find a better balance.

But I couldn't dwell on it for too long, prospective pet owners began to come look at the puppies and then more to see me, the one and only Liam Gaffney up close and personal. I didn't expect so many people to know I was here since I agreed at what I thought was last minute. I guess that was the power of social media and the internet. It was so easy to spread the word. We sold out of the pre-signed shirts within thirty minutes and were more than halfway through the personalized shirts by the time we hit the hour and a half mark.

"Can I get you a coffee or a hand massage?" Abigail asked jokingly.

"I'll take both please." I winked. It was fun to flirt with a woman who wasn't a fan. It was refreshing, and I was excited to talk to her about Chaucer at some point.

Arlene, who had been leaning on a corner wall behind

us, reading a contract on her phone, and probably spying on me to make sure everything went well, called out to us. "I'll make a Starbucks run. I saw one down the street when we were driving in. Can I get you anything, Abi?" Arlene liked Abigail, I could tell. Especially since she felt comfortable leaving me with her for the time it would take to do a Starbucks run.

Abigail gave Arlene a thankful smile. "Are you sure? It's been so crazy here this morning. I don't think I've ever seen it this busy."

Although it had only been a couple of hours, it was a jam packed adoption event. I knew she had to be as tired as I was. I gave her arm a jostle "She means it. Leeni never jokes about Starbucks."

"Thanks, I could really use a caffeine fix. I would love a venti iced cinnamon dolce latte, please."

"Coming right up." Arlene smiled. "And I already know what you want." She gave my shoulder a squeeze as she left.

"She must really like you," I commented.

Abigail grabbed my signing hand and began to massage it. Bold move on her part I thought. I wonder what had come over her. Whatever it was, I liked it. My insides did a little flip at the warmth and softness of her hands working on mine. "Why do you say that?"

I loved the way Abigail was massaging my hand. I could feel all the cramping from so many rapid-fire sign-ings just start to melt away. She had such a delicate touch and to my surprise it made me tingle. So much so that I had to push away the thought of her hands roaming down my abdomen and took a deep breath, so I could concentrate on the question she had just asked me. "Leenie has been my agent since I started. She's like a big sister to me. She never, and I do mean never, leaves my side when I do events alone. Hence, she likes you. She clearly felt safe leaving me here with you and the puppies."

Abigail gave me a mischievous smile. "How do you feel about kittens?"

"Kittens?"

"Yeah, you must need a break, and the kittens are a little further back in the building. It tends to be quieter back there."

I nod. "Your massage feels really good by the way. My hand feels better already."

Abigail smiled. "I've been told I have magic fingers."

Who was this woman? I wondered. She was bold and shy at the same time. But more bold. I liked it. She seemed very sure of herself. That was such a turn on for me. I hated insecure women. "Oh really?" I raised an eyebrow.

Abigail quickly gave my hand one last pat and then let go. "Come on, let's say hi to the kittens." She stood and I followed her into the kitten room. She picked up a sweet little calico and handed it to me. The kitten immediately crawled up my chest and curled up in the crook of my neck by my shoulder. I could hear a faint purr as it settled itself.

Abigail laughed. "You're stuck with her now, guess you'll have to adopt her."

I gently scratched the little kitten ball that I now knew was a girl. "I guess I will."

Abigail was shocked. "I was only kidding. You don't actually have to adopt her."

I just smiled and shrugged. "I could use the company. Do you have any?"

Abigail nodded. "Two cats, a brother and sister. I've had them since they were kittens. They are three years old now. I got them from here actually."

I should have known she was an animal lover, otherwise why would she volunteer here? "Two? Really? What are their names?"

~ ABIGAIL ~

S hit! He wanted to know their names! I had to think quickly. Maybe I could distract him with a non-answer, answer. "Uh, yes. I was only going to get one, but then I didn't want her to be alone while I was at work, so I got her brother too."

"And their names?" Liam asked again.

Before I could answer, a group of girls came in asking for photos. Liam graciously took selfies with all of them. The cat never moved. It gave me a moment to think, and I had to think fast. I couldn't very well tell him that my cats were named Lochlan and Beatrice. The stifled giggles and squeals getting farther and farther away told me my time was up. I needed to give him an answer. I waited until the entire group filed out. "I named them Cassieopia and Dipper, after my two favorite constellations."

"Ah, you're a star gazer are you?"

I smiled. "Among other things."

"I'd like to hear more about the other things."

I was stunned. Was Liam flirting with me? And if so,

was it a genuine flirt or a television personality flirt? And was there even a difference? I guessed there had to be a difference. And I guess I had started flirting first right? Even if it had been unintentional. Or was it? I wasn't even sure anymore. This whole day had felt like something I was watching, not living.

"Maybe we could have dinner together?" Liam interrupted my thoughts.

"Sure that would be very nice," I squeaked out. Damn it! My nerves were betraying my voice.

Liam looked surprised I had said yes. I assumed most women said yes to him. Was he actually worried that I might have said no?

"Can I pick you up at seven? That will give me time to freshen up and set up my new roommate here. Maybe you can help me figure out a name for her at dinner."

I nodded. "Seven sounds great." I had found my voice again.

"What sounds great?" Arlene asked as she handed each of us an iced coffee. "I couldn't find you for a minute, but then I saw a crowd of giggling young women coming back from this way and I figured it was a safe bet."

"Abi here has agreed to have dinner with me. And I've decided to adopt this little beauty here on my shoulder." Liam smiled.

Arlene was quiet for a moment but quickly recovered. "I think that's a great idea. Well, the dinner, not sure about the cat. Um, Liam, can I talk to you privately for a moment?"

~ LIAM ~

Arlene walked me over to a quiet corner in the room. I could tell she had put her big sister hat on.

"What's up?" I asked as I tried to remove the calico from my shoulder. She just doubled down and began to purr louder so I left her there.

"Do you really think that dinner is a good idea?"

I shrugged. "I like Abi. She's great to be around. I can relax around her, it's really quite nice. Besides, it's just dinner, and I'm hoping she can answer some questions about *The Canterbury Tales* for me."

"About that, I got a call today. The role is yours if you want it. I still need to iron out some things in your contract but it's all yours." Arlene smiled. "You just can't tell anyone yet."

I grabbed her into a hug lifting her off the ground for a moment. My six foot stature was no match for her small five foot four frame. "You are the best!" I whispered. "But of course mums the word. I know better than to say anything."

"So your Chaucer conversation at dinner?"

I chuckled, "Remember, this isn't my first rodeo. The conversation will be about the book and finding a name for this beauty on my shoulder. Speaking of, would you mind getting her on my flight with me? And maybe pick up a small litter box and some food? I'll gather the good stuff when I get home."

"You mean home to the city you are filming in and will be leaving in four months to go shoot somewhere else for two months?"

My shoulders slumped. "But she's so cute."

"Look, I'll make the arrangements and pick up some things to last you until the flight if you really want me to, but you need to really think this through."

"I already told Abi I was taking her." I winced, waiting for Arlene's lecture.

I was surprised when a big smile slowly crept across Arlene's face. "Well, well, well. I believe you are turning into a smitten kitten right before my eyes."

"Stop, Leenie." I rolled my eyes.

"No, no, there is a glint in those eyes I haven't seen in a while. Did I mention that *Tales* is filming only an hour from this lovely little Connecticut town?"

I couldn't control my smile. "Leenie, can you help me out or not?"

"Of course." Arlene nodded as she made a note in her phone. "Do you know where you want to take her for dinner?"

I looked at her with a sweet smile and batted my eyes. "I have no idea. Maybe you could—"

She wagged a finger at me. "Boy! You're lucky I love you!" I'll see what I can find." Arlene looked over at Abigail. She was helping a guest pick out the perfect kitten. It was obvious she was great with children.

"You do realize the two of you will be all over twitter and Instagram if you take her out tonight. I mean of course today's function will be, but dinner is an entirely different ballgame. Is she ready for that?"

I looked over at Abigail. It had snuck up on me, but I realized I felt happy. Could it be that my heart was beginning to soften again after my hurtful and very public breakup with my former co-star Bianca Monroe two years ago? Bianca hadn't been my first humiliating public break up. But she was certainly going to be the last. I shook my head, enough with the dark memories. Thankfully Arlene didn't give me another minute to think about it.

"Hey, just do me a favor. Don't stay out too late. We both have early morning flights, and I promised the show you'd be ready for a short night shoot when you got back. No dialogue. Just that fight scene in the water you were rehearsing all last week."

I nodded and crossed my heart. "Scouts honor. Relax, it's just dinner. It's not like I'm asking her to marry me."

Arlene shook her head. She wasn't as sure of that as I was. "Okay, if you say so. I'll see what I can come up with."

"You really are the best!" I gave her a kiss on the cheek. "And I'm keeping the kitten." I gave Arlene a wink and walked back over to Abigail.

~ ABIGAIL ~

The adoption day had been long but worth it. Liam's shirts alone raised almost five thousand dollars. And in total we had raised more money than any previous year. I flopped on the couch smiling to myself thinking about Liam adopting that sweet little calico.

I felt a little bit guilty since I had suggested it, well implied it really. Forced him maybe? I shook off the feeling. He could have said no at any time. I cuddled Lochlan and Beatrice as I thought about what I wanted to wear.

I started laughing uncontrollably. My somewhat hysterical laugh scared Beatrice and Lochlan enough that they scampered off the couch and into another room. I had a date, and not just any date, but a date with Liam Caffney. The sixteen year old fangirl deep inside me was doing the happy dance. However the moment didn't last long as a sense of panic came over me.

My mind began to run a mile a minute on what could or couldn't happen. That it could be wonderful or a complete disaster, or worse, come off like one big joke. Rubbing my eyes, I tried to clear my head. I needed to get a grip. Everything was going to be fine. I headed to the shower to get clean and relax. That way I'd have a clear head to figure out what I would wear.

I had no idea where we were going, and I didn't want to be overdressed or underdressed. I wanted something that showed off my curves but wasn't necessarily sexy, but I didn't want to be frumpy. I shook my head and laughed. None of my clothes were frumpy. I was very meticulous about that. It was hard enough to find decent plus size clothes so when I found a good source, I allowed myself the indulgence of the exorbitant prices the store gouged me, and other plus size beauties out of. It was extortion, plain and simple. But it's just the way things were. Beatrice and Lochlan were snoozing on my bed. I gave them each a rub to the ears as I headed to the shower. Music blasting, I cleaned myself up.

Hands on hips, draped in a towel, I stared at my clothes, willing the perfect outfit to reveal itself. "By the Goddess of Nyla and all the realm, I need a great outfit!" I shouted into the air. I sighed. But then like the magic of the fae, an outfit materialized in my mind. I flipped through the hangers looking for the blouse and pants I had imagined. Why hadn't I thought of it sooner? I prayed they weren't wrinkled. But if they were, I had time to steam it. They would be perfect, I hoped.

I took a deep breath and one last look in the mirror before I left my house. We were meeting at one of my favorite Italian Bistros. I was surprised he had chosen it since it was on a main strip downtown. This being a Saturday, it was sure to be busy.

The thought made me stop in my tracks. Was this just a publicity opportunity for him? Taking the girl he volunteered with, out for a meal. Was I just more charity work for him? I laughed as I slapped my cheeks softly several times. I was letting my paranoia show through. This wasn't like me, losing my self confidence. I chastised myself for the momentary lapse. This was nothing more than extending the interesting and fun time we had this afternoon. Nothing more and nothing less. And he wanted to talk Chaucer.

Arlene had arranged for us to meet at the restaurant, instead of having me pick Abigail up. I swallowed hard and rubbed the sweat from my palms as I saw Abigail walk up. Her braids were down, unlike this afternoon when they were in a high ponytail. They fell around her face in a way that was captivating to me.

I had only just arrived but wanted to wait outside for her. I gave her a hug as she reached the door. "You look wonderful."

I looked Abigail up and down smiling at her outfit choice. She had on a pair of black slacks that had an intricate knot design in a very thin cream colored thread. It could be missed if the light didn't hit it just the right way. For the top she had chosen a cream, deep scoop neck sleeveless top that showed off her cleavage nicely as well as a lovely necklace. It was the kind of shirt that hugged in all the right places. Her shoes were a simple black ankle boot with a heel that was about half an inch. I wondered if she just wasn't a heel person or was it because of the winter months when snow and ice were possible. Either way, she looked fashionable yet comfortable.

"Thank you. You clean up pretty nice yourself." Abigail smiled at me.

I hadn't planned on having a nice dinner out while I was in town. I thought room service would be my best mate. This was an in and out trip. Thankfully, Arlene had come to my rescue and picked me up a v-neck long sleeve shirt that had just a little heft to it to keep me warm, in a shade of green that made my eyes sparkle even more. Black pants were a staple in my wardrobe, so I had been safe there. I chuckled as I realized I also had black boots on. But my boots weren't ankle length, they would be considered calf length. Doc Martin's were my favorite, but no heel for me.

"Before we go in, I just wanted to make sure that you are okay with getting your picture taken. I'm sorry, I should have asked earlier, but I can guarantee if you walk in there with me, and have a meal with me, your photo will be taken and displayed who knows where."

Abigail nodded. "It's fine, it's not like we'll be walking out of a hotel room or anything," she joked. "It's just dinner."

I could see the thought had crossed her mind at some point between the time I asked her to dinner and now. From what she had seen today she must have figured it out that it would be inevitable. I was hoping she also knew it would blow over quickly as this was a one time thing and there would be something bigger and better to gossip about by Monday. Laughing, I nodded. "That's pretty much what I told Leenie, but I just wanted to double check with you first." He opened the door to the restaurant. "Shall we?"

Abigail stepped in and up to the host stand. I moved up next to her and smiled at the young hostess who looked like she had just seen a ghost. "Hello there, you should have a reservation for two under the name Wheems."

The hostess nodded as she looked for the name, and nodded again as she crossed it off the list and grabbed two menus. "Just follow me please." She sat us at the table and handed Abigail her menu first. As she handed me mine, she leaned in and whispered, "I love you on the show," then scurried away quickly.

Abigail watched her go. "Why did she -"

I waved my hand as if it was nothing. "She would have gotten in trouble if her manager saw her do that. It's happened before."

Abigail smiled. "So it seems you're reading my mind now. Okay, swamy, what am I wondering now?"

I took her hand in mine, closed my eyes and stroked her hand several times before speaking. "You are wondering why the reservation was under the last name Wheems. You're wondering if that is my real last name, or just the name I use when making reservations."

Abigail gently pulled her hand away. "Okay, now you're freaking me out."

I laughed. "Wheems is Leenie's last name."

"That's Arlene right? I thought I heard you call her Leenie today."

I nodded. "Yup, it's my nickname for her. It helps from keeping too many looky loos coming in or making reservations at the same time to catch a glimpse."

Abigail cocked her head, raising an eyebrow. "You have my sympathy?"

"I know, I know, first world problems. I do keep it in perspective though. I promise."

That answer seemed to satisfy Abigail. She sat back and started looking at the menu. The server came over and filled our water glasses and then asked, "Can I get you any appetizers this evening?"

I looked at Abigail. She just shrugged. I took another look at the menu. "Can we get an order of stuffed mushrooms and an order of calamari please. Oh and a bottle of Vineyard West Petite Syrah."

The server nodded. "I'll put that right in for you and then come back with your drinks. My name is Matthew." He gave us both a nod and walked away.

I looked at Abigail. Her amber eyes had a richness to them, with just a swirl of gold, it was almost hypnotic. I blinked, realizing I had stared a moment too long. "I hope you don't mind what I ordered."

"Not at all! And that is actually one of my favorite wines. But how did you discover it? I'm assuming from that amazing accent, the U.S. is not your home."

"You think my accent is amazing, do you?" I winked.

Abigail was slightly flustered, but she recovered quickly. "You know the old saying, women are always suckers for accents."

"I wouldn't call you a sucker, but I'm glad you like my accent. But to answer your question I've lived in Manhattan, when I'm not off filming, for about six years now. So I found the wine somewhere along the way there. A lot of places carry it, which makes me happy."

"Shut up! I lived in Manhattan for undergrad and grad

school. I moved up here when I got offered a teaching position."

"Didn't want to teach in the big bad city?"

"Ha! No, it was time for me to go. I wanted a little more nature and a little less concrete."

Liam nodded. "Understandable, to be honest with my work schedule, I've been there maybe a total of two years timewise with all the traveling I do with work."

"And you adopted a kitten?! Sorry, that didn't come out the way I meant it to." A look of guilt swept across Abigail's face.

I needed to get that look of guilt out of her eyes. I chuckled and put my hand over hers. I was taken aback by how much I liked touching her. The physical contact was stirring something within me. Something I hadn't felt in a very long time. I leaned in, wanting to get closer to her. "Now you sound just like Leenie. She's worried I won't have time for -" I sat up and leaned back a little. I was getting too close and I had to remember where I was, and what this was. "You know, I still don't have a name for her. Will you help me think of one?"

~ ABIGAIL ~

Liam was looking directly in my eyes. I felt my pulse begin to quicken a little and all of a sudden, my mouth became dry. I loved looking in his eyes. As I blinked I still couldn't believe this was happening. But what was happening? Was he feeling the same heat, the same chemistry I was? Or was it all in my wonderfully dirty imagination? The answer was nothing, nothing was happening, it was just dinner. I remembered he asked me a question that needed an answer. "Um, sure, sure."

Matthew came back with our wine, breaking the moment. He took our dinner order promising the appetizers shortly and left us alone again. Before we could resume our conversation a woman about my age came up to the table. "I'm so sorry to bother you. But I just had to tell you how much I enjoy watching you on *EverMorphs*. Would you mind signing an autograph for me?" She handed him a clean cloth napkin she had grabbed off the empty table next to us.

Liam gave the woman one of his best smiles, much like the one he had given Simone earlier today "That's so kind of you to say. Of course I will, my darlin' what's your name?"

"My name is Monica." She looked me up and down and gave me a little half smile, that actually looked more like a sneer. "Is this your girlfriend?"

I was stunned at the audacity of this woman, this stranger, to ask someone she really didn't know such a personal question. It took all of my will power not to give her a piece of my mind about boundaries. But Liam seemed to take it in stride.

"Oh no! I've never been lucky enough to call this one my girl. She's a dear friend I've known since before I hit puberty. Maybe one day I'll be lucky enough to call her my gal." Liam blew me a kiss and winked at me.

He didn't see the full on dirty look Monica gave me as he was signing the napkin. To no one's surprise she had a sharpie in her purse. Monica changed her tune as Liam was finishing up. "Thank you so much. I'll let you get back to your dinner. It was wonderful to meet you." Monica stroked and squeezed his shoulder as she walked away. She'd only taken two steps before she whipped out her phone and quickly took a picture. We both could see the flash out of the corner of our eyes. And we both chose to ignore it.

"I cannot believe you said that! Did you see the dirty look she gave me?!"

Liam stifled a laugh. "I'm sorry Abi, I couldn't resist. I've met that woman so many times and given her photos and autographs up the wazoo. I really didn't think I would run into her here. And if she realized that I recognized her, she would have been here another twenty minutes taking a walk down memory lane."

"She sounds like a super fan. I know the event today was supposed to be advertised. Maybe she was there too. You know that photo is probably already up on her Instagram page."

"Or her twitter feed." Liam snickered.

"Ha ha sir! Very funny." I shook my head.

The waiter brought over our food and refilled our wine glasses before departing again.

"So, the way you said super fan. Sounded like there was some disdain in your voice." Liam took a bite of his food, acting like his question wasn't a ticking bomb waiting to go off.

I took a large sip of my wine. I needed a moment to think how I was going to answer him. "No, Not really, it was just an observation." I shrugged trying to be nonchalant.

"An observation you didn't like." Liam was pushing.

"I just am not a fan of being a *fan* of anything really. Let alone a *super fan*."

"Super fan were your words, not mine."

I was uncomfortable with the conversation, and I really didn't want to get into my issues with being a fan with the likes of Liam Caffney. "Can we change the subject please? We really need to find a name for your kitten."

"I'm sorry if I upset you. Of course a name is definitely in order." Liam's facial expression told me he knew there was something more there, but that it wasn't the time or place to push.

"Maybe you should give her an Irish name. Something

to remind you of home." I smiled trying to lighten a mood I had made heavy.

Liam grinned. "That's a really good idea. It has been too long since I have been able to make a trip home."

"Maybe you can go after *EverMorphs* finishes filming. Arlene mentioned you were still filming?"

Liam nodded. "I would, but I might have another project that would start too soon for me to go back home. Maybe after that and before the next season of *EverMorphs* starts up again."

"Sounds like you never have much down time."

"No, I don't. But gotta keep busy while the public still *wants* to see my face. I'm thankful for the work."

"You're really quite talented."

~ LIAM ~

"Ah-ha! So you have seen *EverMorphs!*" I smirked. Even if she was a fan I already liked her, I was only teasing. But I liked the idea that she had seen the show at least once. Even if she might not have liked it.

To my disappointment, Abigail shook her head. "Sorry to disappoint you, but I actually saw you in a movie. I can't remember the name, but it was filmed in black and white and you played a pianist who was losing his sight. You were brilliant, I cried." Abigail took another sip of wine.

I wasn't sure if she had really forgotten the name of the movie but I was going to take her at her word. "It was called Keys. I loved everything about that movie. I even learned how to play the piano for the role. I'm no Mozart, but I can play a tune well." I wiped a bit of butter off the corner of my mouth and put my napkin back in my lap. "I think I'm going to go with Aoife. It means beautiful, like you." I took a long drink, letting my heartbeat slow down. I hadn't expected to say that, it kind of just slipped out. I really hoped she didn't think I was being phony with her like I had been with Monica, or that I was being too forward.

"I think that's a lovely name. I'm sure you'll be very happy with her, and she will give you lots of love."

I couldn't tell if she was blushing, her sable skin hid any shade of pink that would rise to her cheeks. And she made no comment about what I said about her. "So tell me Abi, when you are not working at the shelter or teaching English, what do you like to do?"

"Well, I really like to write. Sometimes poems, but mostly fiction."

I was intrigued. "Short stories or novels? Have you ever tried to publish anything?"

"Oh no, I just do it for myself. Once upon a time I thought of being an author, it just wasn't meant to be. But I love teaching, and I still have time to write. Even if I'm the only one who reads it."

"Well I'd love to read something you wrote. I love to read."

"Really? What are you reading now?"

"Oddly enough, *The Canterbury Tales*."

Abigail tried to keep her wine in as she laughed out loud. "Are you serious? You're just saying that!"

"No, no, it's true. I picked it up and was reading it on the plane. It's sitting on the night table in my hotel room right now. If I'm honest I'm actually having a bit of trouble with it."

"I'd be happy to help you with it if you want. It's kinda what I do." Abigail smiled.

I reached across and squeezed her hand. "That would be wonderful. I'd really like that." If she helped me that would mean I'd be able to spend more time with her, at the very least video chat with her.

She squeezed my hand back and nodded. "Okay, so when you aren't acting, or reading, or cuddling your brand new kitten, what do you like to do? What would you be if you weren't an actor?"

I leaned back in my chair. "Oh, such a loaded question. Shall we discuss it over dessert?" I waved the waiter over. I ordered Tiramisu for both of us along with some tea. As Matthew was walking away I looked at Abigail. "Oh, I'm sorry, I did it again. I ordered for both of us. I hope that's okay."

"Well, I did order my own choice for the main dish. And your appetizer choices were wonderful, so I think it's cute that you ordered for both of us. As a long time friend, I have to say you really know how to treat a lady." Abigail winked at me. We both began to laugh. "But seriously, you aren't an actor, what are you? Go!" Abigail just looked at me as she swirled the remaining wine in her glass.

"I guess I would say a photographer. I've been into photography since I was young. My aunt got me a camera for my twelfth birthday. At least I think it was my twelfth birthday. Anyway, I've been taking pictures ever since. I've even framed a couple of them over the years, given some as gifts."

"I have a proposition for you." A sly smile appeared on Abigail's lips.

I leaned into the table with a raised eyebrow. I almost reached for her hand again but fought the urge. "Oh really?"

"I'll show you mine if you show me yours."

~ ABIGAIL ~

Who was I right now? Was it the wine making me so bold, or was it the man? Either way, I regretted my words almost the second it came out of my mouth. It was such a loaded statement, and I didn't mean it the way it sounded. I mean I would love to see him—no! I needed to stop thinking like that. He was too good at reading my thoughts. He was very good with context clues.

"Why Abi, you little minx!" he chortled.

I let out a nervous giggle. "I meant I'll show you something I wrote if you share some of your photography."

"I know what you meant. I just like teasing you." Liam winked. "I would be honored to read some of your work. And I'll gladly share some of my photography. Just be kind please."

"Same to you."

We finished our dessert and tea as we discussed places we had traveled, favorite books we had read, and the toughest crossword puzzle we had ever finished in ink.

The evening ended far too soon for my liking and I had an inkling of a feeling that Liam felt the same way. Liam paid, leaving Matthew a very generous tip. He opened the door for me, being a true gentleman.

"May I walk you to your car?"

"Of course. Thank you."

Liam laced his hand in mine as we walked. Such a simple act made me giddy. It warmed my entire body from head to toe. It was a long forgotten warmth but a pleasant one. I squeezed his hand trying to convey my feelings without words, because I didn't know everything I was feeling, or how to process it all right now. So instead I decided to be in the present, to enjoy the feeling of Liam's warm hand, the beat of his pulse against mine. I started to walk slower to prolong the moment. But in a few more short steps, we were standing by my car.

Liam took a step closer as he wrapped his arms around my waist letting them rest gently on my ass. He didn't caress it. Just let his fingers graze against it. "Abi, can I ask you a question?"

"Of course," I barely whispered.

"May I kiss you? I feel, fuck, I don't know what I feel. I just know I will regret it if I—"

I didn't let him finish his sentence, I reached up and kissed him. I let my lips melt into his as he tightened his grasp on me. He caressed my ass as he deepened his kiss, and I opened my mouth to him. I ran my hands along his back and up to his neck, playing with his curls at the nape. We got lost in the moment, not aware of our surroundings anymore. My head was spinning in the most delicious way, our hearts beating fast. Liam finally began to pull back. He quickly looked around, as if he was looking for someone. I looked around as well but there wasn't anyone near us. If someone had been there before he wouldn't have noticed.

I stepped back, as my heart sank. Was he regretting the kiss? Was it too public? This was all wrong. How could I have been so stupid? I fumbled around in her purse for her keys. Liam grabbed my hand.

"Hey, are you okay? Did I overstep?"

My keys slipped out of my hands onto the concrete. I couldn't look Liam in the eye. I just looked down at my fallen keys. "Are you embarrassed that you kissed me? Do you regret it?"

Liam placed his thumb and forefinger on my chin lifting it up so I was looking him in the eyes."God no! Why would you say that?"

"Because you're looking around like you don't want to be seen with me all of a sudden." I did everything not to cry. I hated that I cried not only when I was sad but when I was angry. And right now I was angry and embarrassed. However I refused to cry in front of Liam Caffney.

Liam pulled me into a hug. "No, it's not that. I was just checking to see if anybody had taken a photo. I don't regret kissing you, please believe that." He clasped my face in his hands. "But this first kiss, this first amazing kiss, which I hope will only be the beginning, I want *that* kiss to have been just for us."

I really didn't know what to make of all of this. But I did believe him. I just had no idea what this could all mean for the two of us and what would come next. He kissed me again, pressing me against my car. He held my neck in place as he deepened his kiss, biting my lower lip before sucking on my tongue.

"I really should go. I have an early morning flight."

Liam whispered as he licked my ear. "But I don't want to go, but I also don't want to be a cad and invite you back to my hotel."

"I wouldn't go if you asked." I grinned.

Liam chuckled as he kissed my neck. "That's just another reason I like you. Liam took a step back, picked up my keys, and handed them to me.

"Can I give you a ride to your hotel?" I asked. It would give me just a little more time with him.

"I'd like nothing more."

~ ABIGAIL ~

I was in a world of my own, recounting every moment of the last several hours. I nearly jumped out of my skin as I screamed with mace in hand when my living room light went on as I was locking the front door behind me.

"Lucy! You gotta lot of esplaning to do!" yelled my best friend Tess in the worst Ricky Ricardo accent possible.

"Dammit Tess! I almost maced you! What are you doing here!" I put my purse down on the kitchen table.

"Well, you didn't answer your phone and I had to know exactly what the hell this is all about!" Tess showed me a picture on her phone. It was one of the many fan pages for *EverMorphs* and there, front and center, was a picture of Liam and I in the restaurant laughing over something. "I don't know what stuns me more, the fact that you went to dinner with the super hot Liam Caffney or that you didn't tell your best friend in the entire world that it was happening!"

"God! I never should have given you a key. It's supposed to be for emergencies."

"My best friend going on a date with Liam Caffney *is* an emergency."

I flung my boots off, and went to fill my tea kettle with water. "I was going to call you the minute I got home. Would you like some tea?"

"Tea?" Tess got up and came into the kitchen. "Got anything stronger?"

I shook my head. "If I drink any more tonight, I won't be able to drink at brunch tomorrow. I had a lot of wine tonight." I set my tea box on the table. "In fact, if we could table this discussion until tomorrow that would be great. I'm beat." I gave my friend a hug and headed to my bedroom, and closed the door behind me.

Tess promptly opened it. "Nope, you're not getting off that easy. We can skip brunch if you are too tired, but you are telling me everything that happened, and you are telling me now."

I sighed, I knew she wouldn't go quietly. "Fine, can I just put my pajamas on first please?"

Tess whipped out an overnight bag she had lying by the coffee table. "Ha! A sleepover! You fell right into my trap. Go change, I'll change out here and make some popcorn.

I had to laugh, Tess always got what she wanted. Her tenacity was one of my favorite things about her, except when it was used against me. I washed the makeup off my face and changed into my favorite pair of yellow striped jammy bottoms with a yellow sleep tank. I put my braids back in a loose ponytail so they wouldn't be flying around in my face. I smiled remembering how Liam had gently moved them out of my face when we were talking by my car. And again when he kissed me goodnight.

"Hey! Are you okay in there?" Tess knocked loudly on the door.

I put my game face on and headed out to the living room. Even though she was my best friend, I wasn't sure just how much I wanted to share yet. Tess had set out popcorn and two cups of mint-lavender tea. She wrapped me in a great big hug. That was all I needed, I don't know what came over me. Maybe it was all the adrenaline leaving my body but I started to cry.

"Oh Abi! Don't cry. What's wrong? I thought you would be on cloud nine right now."

"I don't know why I'm crying. It was a great night really, he kissed me! And I really really liked it!" I started crying harder.

Tess guided me over to the couch and sat me down. "Honey, you're not making any sense." She handed me some tea.

I explained everything that happened from the time Liam arrived at the shelter until I walked into my apartment to find Tess waiting there. The entire time Tess listened, giving me her full attention and eating popcorn like she was watching a *Lifetime* movie.

"Holy shit, Abi. Like seriously holy shit!"

"I know, I know. But what do I do now? Maybe I do nothing. I mean it's not like he asked for my number."

"Alright, let's look at this logically. Liam doesn't live in this state. He travels for work all the time and is gone months and months at a stretch. What tonight was should be chalked up to just a beautiful moment in time. Don't try to think ahead or about the future. Especially since he doesn't even know what you are."

"You make me sound inhuman with your '*he doesn't know what you are*' talk."

Tess laughed. "I was just talking about the 'F' word. He doesn't know you are one."

"I think it would change everything if he did." I hung my head. "I hate this! I never should have agreed to be his handler during the pet event. If I had just kept my distance, none of this would have happened."

"But it did. So as I see it, you have a couple of choices. One, come clean that you are a fan of his and a fan of the show."

I shook my head as I made a face at Tess. "I don't like that option. You know how I feel about that word. It's just as bad as a swear word. It leaves a bad vibe in the air and people treat you differently once it comes out of your mouth. What else do you have?"

Tess took a sip of her tea. "You could just go with the flow and see what happens. Pray the truth will never come out."

"But the truth always comes out, doesn't it?" I sighed.

Tess nodded. "Yes, yes it most certainly does."

I tried to keep the feeling of dread at bay. "Tess, I don't even know why we are discussing this. It's a moot point. It's like you said. He's not even from here. It was a glorious moment in time that I will cherish for the rest of my life. It was the best 'meeting your celebrity crush' experience I could have wished for."

"But you told me he asked for your help with Chaucer. That means there will be more contact."

I shrugged. "For all I know he was just being nice. If he

meant it, he would have asked for my phone number or at the very least my email address. That didn't happen, end of story."

Tess looked at me. As my bestie she could read me better than anyone. The way she was looking at me I knew she wasn't sure if she believed me. Her gut told her there was more to my story. She just wasn't sure how it would end.

~ LIAM ~

I knew I was being extra quiet on the plane ride back to Toronto. I just stared out the window, with Aoife safely stowed under my seat. I looked over at Arlene, she was on her laptop emailing a client no doubt. She had been in the game only a little longer than me. I was one of her first clients. Since then she's picked up many more clients and a lot of us work on shows that are filmed in Toronto and Vancouver. I'd say she spends more time traveling between us and her office in New York, than actually in New York. But her personal touch was one of the reasons she was so successful.

Arlene finished her email, closed her laptop and tapped me on the shoulder. "Penny for your thoughts."

"I'm just a little tired, Leenie."

"Do you want to talk about it?"

I smiled at Arlene. "You think I have something to talk about?"

"I think you need to talk about your date. I mean, it was a date, right?"

I couldn't keep the giant smile from crossing my face. "And a glorious one at that."

"So, what's the problem?"

"Well, for one, she's a civilian. The thought of throwing her into the spotlight, I don't know if that's fair to her."

Arlene snorted. "Trust me when I say she can hold her own. So that doesn't count. What else have you got?"

"I don't live anywhere near her?"

"Technically you only live one state, one train ride away."

"And I'm never home."

"Okay, you got me there. But listen Liam, in the short time I saw you with her, and make no mistake I had eagle eyes on you the whole time, your entire demeanor changed in a way I haven't seen in a very long time. It's worth investigating."

"Maybe?"

"She got you to get a kitten for Christ sake! I think it's worth a moment of your time to see what it could be."

I put my arm around Arlene, giving her a side hug. "Leenie, you are the big sister I never wanted." He kissed her cheek. "Thank you."

"Well, I have some news that will make things a little easier for you, I hope. I have a wonderful contract for you to sign, and then it will be official. You will officially be the Pardoner on *Hidden Tales*."

I leaned back in his seat and smiled. "Thank you, Leenie. You're the best." I closed my eyes and began to relax.

"Should I tell you I looked into Abi's background? You know, just in case."

I shot up in my seat. Eyes wide open. "You did what?!"

Arlene held her hands up like it was a stick up. "Don't be mad. I was just being careful. Besides, I didn't find anything terrible. She has a private Instagram page, no Facebook or Twitter to speak of, and her LinkedIn is all about her teaching."

"I don't want to hear any more about this. You shouldn't have done that." I whispered, teeth clenched, jaw set.

Arlene squeezed my hands. "Okay, okay. I won't mention it again."

I looked at Arlene. "Nothing terrible? But you did find something."

Arlene opened her mouth to speak but I shut her down.

"Nope!" I leaned back again and put my earbuds in, and shut my eyes. I was done talking for the duration of the flight.

AND THAT'S ALL I HAVE TO SAY ABOUT THAT!

ALL THINGS EVERMORPH ALL THE TIME

SEASON 4

Episode Highlight: the BIG reveal of
who was spying on Lochlan and Beatrice!
Episode Lowlight: Where the hell is
Flint!!!

*Greetings Everrites and Morphlings. WOW! Just WOW!! This
week's episode was in one word, AMAZING. Try to tell me
differently! Go ahead! Try! You can't, can you? I knew it!!
Alright, let us bask in the awe and wisdom of the episode for a
moment. For all of you who thought it was Nyx spying, you are
the big winners. But did you see what she turned into? Am I the
only one who didn't know that maiden fairies could transform
into warrior elfkins!? What kind of weird hybrid breeding
makes that possible? I need some serious backstory on that one
please! I mean she freaking bit Lochlan! If Beatrice hadn't hit
her from behind, I really think she would have bit that arm*

clean off! Thank the Goddess Beatrice has all that medical training (wink wink).

    BUT, where the hell was Flint? Isn't he supposed to be Lochlan's right hand man, best friend, and most importantly HIS PROTECTOR?!? Yes, yes, they were having a relatively private moment, but Flint should be within earshot. ESPE-CIALLY if Lochlan is venturing into the human world! He better have been kidnapped by Oberon, or being seduced by Zarina. I think those are the only two reasons I will accept at this moment. What about you? Come on Fae folk, share your thoughts and comments.

    Until next time EternallyEvers OUT!!

COMMENTS:

> NyxIsMySpiritGuide: Hell yeah Nyx was spying! I'm hoping her actions will show Isla how much she really loves her.

> > NylaKingdom4Ever Sorry but Isla will never leave Lochlan. She loves him. Even with his actions of late.

> RogansRaiders: That transformation was awesome! I'm with you EE I want some serious back story on that!

> Morphing4Oberon: Something bad is definitely happening with Flint. He would NEVER leave Lochlan unprotected.

> LochlanIsMine: Lochlan will find Flint, I mean once he's done flirting with Beatrice. LOL

"**M**iss Reese!" Jacob raised his hand urgently.

"Yes, Jacob?" I asked as I wrote some of my famous 'think for a moment' questions on the board about the reading from the weekend homework assigned. I usually wasn't one of those teachers who regularly assigned weekend homework. I wanted my students to have their weekends free to pursue hobbies and other interests like I did. But the past weekend had required a little reading because my students just weren't picking up Chaucer as easily or as quickly as I had hoped.

"This assignment. I got so frustrated. I had to stop and start at least ten times. There has got to be an easier way." A wave of murmurs of agreement swept across the room.

I turned to my students. "Okay, alright, time for a ring of truth." I went to my filing cabinet and pulled out a bag of tootsie pops. "Everyone, shoes off and take a seat on top of the desks." I placed one Tootsie pop on every desk and then went to the middle of the figure eight. "You all are intelligent human beings and because I respect you, I do not want to dumb down Chaucer for you. I want you to be challenged, even pushed a little. But I don't want it to get so frustrating for you that you completely give up. So, we are going to try a couple of different things. But before we do any of that, do any of you have any questions I could help you with right now?"

Several hands shot up in the air. I sighed a little internally. My head exploding sticker was coming to fruition way too soon in the segment. I pointed to Amanda. "Yes Amanda?"

"Did you go on a date with Liam Caffney this past weekend?"

"Shut up," Margot shrieked "For real?"

Amanda nodded "Yes! See?" Amanda pulled a fan page for *EverMorphs* on Instagram and handed her phone to Margot. She swooned over the photos and then handed the phone to Rebecca who also swooned and handed it off to someone else.

"No phones in my class, Amanda! You know the rules."

"Wait, is he the dude from the TV show with all the fairies? My sister loves that crap." Keith laughed as his turn to view the pictures came around.

"Forget your little sister, I love that show and Lochlan is my favorite!" Amy exclaimed.

"He did that action movie with Ross Gander! I read he did all his own stunts. Well the ones the studio would allow him to do anyway," Robbie chimed in.

"He is so hot! I love him on *The EverMorphs*! Are you two like an item now? You know, he hasn't dated since what's her name broke up with him on the red carpet two years ago," Rebecca asked. The phone had now come full circle.

I could see and hear that I had clearly lost the room. Hopefully I could get the room back on track. "Alright! Alright! Rebecca, please give Amanda her phone back. And Amanda, if I see your phone out again, I'm taking it and you won't get it back until your parents come see me to get it."

Amanda reached for her phone that Rebecca was handing to her. "Sorry Miss Reese. But are you? I mean did you?"

I sighed. There was no way around this. Liam had warned me. "Let's just get this out of the way. Yes, Liam Caffeny and I had dinner last Saturday. He is a lovely person who helped do a fundraiser for the animal shelter I volunteer at. He was thanking me for helping him out. I was his chaperone for the event. And that is all there was to it." I tried not to recall our kiss as I told my students it was just dinner. "Of course there were some pictures taken at dinner and that is all you are seeing there. Just a thank you dinner. Now, we really need to get back to *Canterbury Tales*. Everyone please take out your copy and—"

My room intercom buzzed. I removed myself from the middle of the figure eight and picked up the room phone. "Yes."

"Ms. Reese, will you please come to the office when you have a moment. There is a package down here for you," Estelle, the school secretary, spoke to me.

"Thank you. Can I send a student for it?"

Estelle laughed into the phone. "I don't really think you want your students picking this up for you."

"I'll be down in just a moment, thank you, Estelle." I hung up the phone and turned back to the class. "Okay, I have to run down to the office for a moment. The drama scripts may have arrived. What I want you to do while I am gone is look at the table of contents in *The Canterbury Tales*. Without doing any research or looking up any of the character descriptions, look at the names of each story and write down the name of one that you think will interest you, just by the title alone."

I turned to Margot. "Margot, please collect everyone's answers and put them in the 'pick me' jar and I'll be right back." I closed my classroom door behind me, and I immediately heard loud voices coming from my room discussing the now infamous non-date date. I opened the door and popped my head in, giving them my stern teacher look. "Hey! I expect better from you!" The class immediately quieted down, and I closed the door and headed down to the office.

Estelle was behind her desk typing away when I walked in. I did a quick scan of the counter for my package. I didn't see it. Estelle saw me, but she didn't stop typing, she just motioned with her head to the left. I looked in that direction to find Steve smiling with a very odd sized box in his hands and some flowers on top of the box.

"Hey Abi, this was dropped off at the shelter for you today." Steve smiled. "It came by special courier. I didn't think it could wait until you came in again."

My eyes lit up. I didn't even have to see the label to know it was from Liam. I had no clue what he had sent but I was very curious, and excited. But I stayed in calm teacher mode. I turned to Estelle. "Hey Estelle, can I leave these flowers with you until the end of day? Bringing them up to my classroom will only incur a boat load of questions."

Estelle smiled and nodded. "You mean like who are the flowers from? Or do I even need to ask?"

I shook my head and laughed. "Instagram?"

"Twitter," Estelle replied.

I took the box from Steve. "Thanks for bringing this by."

"Are you going to open it?" Steve wanted to know what Liam had sent as much as I did.

"I think I'll wait until I get home. I'm just going to run this to my car." I turned to Steve. "Steve, I'll walk you out."

"Bell rings in fifteen." Estelle reminded me.

"Shit! Okay, I'll take this with me, and I'll be back for the flowers at the end of the day. Thanks a million, Estelle. I owe you one." I walked Steve as far as the front hall, and gave him a hug. "Thanks again Steve, I really appreciate you dropping this by. I'll call you later and tell you what's inside." I winked. "Maybe." then turned left to head back up to my class.

To my students' credit, they were sitting quietly. Some had their Chaucer books open, others were on their phones. I only needed one guess as to what they were looking up. They quickly squirreled them away then they heard the doorknob. I put the box down behind my desk. "Okay, Margot, let's have that 'pick me' jar." I took the votes out of the jar and counted them twice. "Alright, it looks like we are going to be working on The Pardoner's Tale first. So for now we will be setting aside the syllabus I so painstakingly made."

The class gave me a collective "Aw". They were a bunch of smart asses, but they were my smart asses.

I stifled a snicker. "Tonight I want you to read the first

three stanzas. Then write down what you think each stanza is trying to say. Don't overthink it, just follow the rhythm, the cadence of the piece. Use any context clues you read and most importantly go with your gut. We'll discuss your answers tomorrow." I finished just as the bell rang. The class gathered their things and left.

The rest of the day, I found myself starting each of my classes with 'the Liam question and answer session'. I was glad when the day was finally over. I grabbed my things including my box from Liam before heading down to the office to grab my flowers.

"They really are quite lovely. I got several compliments on them today," Estelle mentioned.

"Thanks for keeping them safe for me Estelle, I really appreciate it." I smiled as I smelled them.

"That must have been some amazing dinner to garnish such a lovely bouquet." Estelle whistled.

I hadn't taken a good look at it before but now that I had time, I could see how elaborate it was. It was full of vibrantly colored flowers and it was a bit of an eclectic bunch. There were roses, peonies, lavender, sunflowers, gerbera daisies, chrysanthemums, lilacs, daffodils, and lilies of the valley. I wasn't even sure if all the flowers were in season at the moment. We hadn't discussed flowers, so he had no idea what my favorites were, but he had managed to get a few of them in there. "It was a lovely dinner." I grinned. "See you tomorrow, Estelle. Thanks again!"

I knew Estelle wanted more details, but Tess was the only person I had any intention of sharing details about Liam and my night with him.

‌ ❖ ❖ ❖ ❖ ❖ ❖

I arrived home and put my things down. I went to change into something more comfortable. I always dressed in style for work, taking great pride in making sure I always looked good. But I also loved a good pair of yoga pants and an oversized tee shirt. Once my comfy clothes were on I headed to the kitchen to see what I wanted to do for dinner.

I opened the fridge and perused what was in there. Nothing spoke to me, or looked appetizing. Sighing, I grabbed her phone and ordered food from my favorite Indian food restaurant.

Sitting on my couch, I turned on the DTV channel. Design Television was my favorite station. I loved any kind of home improvement, house flipping, home building type of shows. A wide smile plastered itself on my face, by this same time next year, I would be ready to start the hunt for my own house. My apartment living days were coming to an end and I couldn't have been more happy. Feeling relaxed, with a glass of wine in hand I finally began to open the box.

I was stunned as I opened the box and peeled away the layers of bubble wrap and tissue. Inside were three framed photos. One was of a sunset over the water, the colors were just brilliant. There was also one of a four leaf clover. It was a close up that looked like it had been captured in the early morning, as there was a drop of dew ready to fall off one of the four leaves.

I was amazed thinking what he had to do to get that shot. The last photo was a black and white of Liam. The

light and shadow made him look almost ethereal. I didn't
even have to ask but I knew he had used a timer and taken
the picture himself. There was something so raw and
sensual about it, I doubted any photographer would have
been able to pull that kind of look out of him. It was a
quiet moment between him, his soul and the camera. I was
honored and humbled that he had shared such an intimate
picture. In the bottom of the box was a card.

I read it out loud, *'I showed you mine, when can I see yours
;) I'd call you, but I don't have your number. So here is mine. Hope
to hear from you - Liam 917- 555- 3663'.* My heart skipped a
beat like it was jumping into a new double dutch game. I
wanted to call him immediately but for a brief moment
wondered if it would make me look desperate. I laughed
before I could even finish the thought. This man had
gotten on a plane back to Toronto and within less than
forty-eight hours had gotten these photos together and
the flowers as well and made sure they found their way
to me.

I looked at the address on the return label. It was a
Canadian address with Arlene's name. It made sense to me
that Liam had put Arlene's address on it. Hell, maybe
Arlene had mailed it for him. Regardless, I now had an
address to *'show him mine'* with. Getting off the couch I
headed for the closet in my bedroom. The best thing
about this apartment besides the amazing balcony was the
extra large master closet. I was able to fit a two drawer
filing cabinet in the closet and it still left plenty of room
for all my other belongings and other bits and baubles I
kept in there.

I was old school in many ways. I wrote all of my stories
and poems with pen and paper before ever dancing my

fingers across a keyboard to memorialize my words in a computer file. I wanted to find the perfect story and poem to send to Liam. Something that matched the intimacy of what he had shared with me.

I made myself comfortable on the floor as I opened the first drawer. I was really proud of some of my earlier pieces but over time I had progressed as a writer and had really hit my stride with some of my later work. After two hours of searching, with a forty minute dinner break, I had settled on one poem and two short stories.

Once picked, I went to my computer and printed out fresh copies, each on different color paper. I carefully used my three hole punch and then bound each one separately with different colored thick ribbons. For the poem I glued a dried flower, a daisy, since the poem was kind of about a daisy. It hung above the title like an umbrella sheltering the poem from the rain. Once they were wrapped in tissue and placed in a box, I wrote a quick note to Liam, sealed the box and addressed it in care of Arlene.

I picked up my phone to call the number. I was about to hit *call* when my mouth got really dry. I took a drink of my wine although that didn't help the dryness, it was helping my nerves. I went to the kitchen and got a glass of water. I downed that and then refilled my wine glass. It was the same kind I had with Liam at dinner. I let my mind wander back to the dinner and was only drawn out by the click of my phone call being connected.I had hit *call* without realizing it. Liam picked up on the second ring.

"Hello?"

"Do you always pick up your phone so quickly?" I smiled into the phone.

"Abi! I was hoping it was you."

I was pleased he remembered my voice so well. "Thank you so much for the photos. They are truly beautiful, and the flowers were as well. They made quite a statement."

"Oh really? What kind of statement?" Liam smiled through the phone.

I got comfortable on the couch, drawing a blanket over me. "Steve dropped them off at my school."

"Ah! Sorry about that. Leenie only knew the address to the shelter."

"Oh don't be! Steve was in all his glory bringing me the box and flowers. He's very invested in the intrigue of it all." I laughed. "And so were my students."

"Oh, no, dare I ask what happened?"

"Just what you mentioned. Photos of us at the restaurant. My students were all over it like white on rice."

"Haha! Sorry, I know I shouldn't laugh." Liam tried to stifle himself.

"No, go ahead, laugh. It was quite comical. I should have expected it. You have quite a few fans among my students."

"Good to know, good to know."

There was something in his voice that worried me, but I couldn't put her finger on it. "I didn't tell them anything if that's what you are concerned about."

"Oh no, I know you wouldn't say anything. I mean if you want to tell them how much I enjoyed kissing you, that's up to you but—"

"Oh no! TMI. I'm their teacher." I laughed as he instantly put me at ease "But you're right. I did enjoy kissing you."

"Mmm, it was lovely, wasn't it? Such soft lips you have. And you smell so good. I can't wait to see you again." Liam almost whispered in a husky yet playful voice. "But anyway, I like that I'm bringing some intrigue into your life. Only time will tell what else I can bring to it."

"I look forward to it."

"So do I. What's that I hear in the background?"

"You can hear that?" I reached for my remote control to turn it down.

"Aye, I've been told I have bat-like hearing."

I couldn't help but laugh. "Me too! My best friend Tess is always telling me that."

"So, what are you watching?"

"I'm watching Design Do-overs on—"

"DTV! I love that channel!! Can't do home improvement to save my life but I love watching all kinds of shows about it!"

Talking with Liam was so easy. There were no awkward pauses. We talked for two hours about everything and nothing at all. I was laughing more in those two hours than I had in the last two months.

"So?" Liam asked with a little mischief in his voice.

"So, what?" I asked.

"When can I see yours?"

"You should see mine in a few days. It's all packed, I'm taking it to FastWay Express tomorrow."

"And then we can discuss my thoughts about it in person."

I sat straight up, my blanket falling down to my feet, landing on Lochlan. He meowed in annoyance as he crawled out from underneath the blanket, and jumped up next to me on the couch. "What do you mean?"

"I have a weekend off in two months. I thought I would come down."

"You'd come all the way down from Toronto. Just to see me?" I could feel my heart begin to race, this was really happening.

"I want to see you again, Abi. Don't you want to see me?"

"More than anything!" I gushed, and then I was silent, forcing my lips not to move so I wouldn't say anything else that sounded stupid. I prayed I didn't sound too eager. It had been a while since I had done this whole flirting, possible relationship thing. I felt like a big ol' fish out of water.

"Abi? Abs? Are you still there?" Liam asked.

"I'm here, I just—"

"So I'll see you in two months?"

"Yes, absolutely."

"I can hear your smile, you know," Liam practically cooed into the phone.

"Right back at you," I responded.

"Maybe pick out a restaurant too? I'd like to take you to your favorite place." Liam offered.

I held my breath for a moment and then let it out. "How about if I cook for you instead?"

"I would love that." Liam said without hesitation.

"Now who's smiling into the phone.?" I laughed.

"I hate to end this lovely conversation, but I have an early call tomorrow." Liam yawned.

"Me too. I have to convince my kids that Chaucer is really awesome to read."

"Sounds like we both have big days tomorrow. Goodnight. I hope you sleep well."

"You too. Goodnight."

~ LIAM ~

Three days later Arlene called me. "I have what appears to be a lovely package for you."

I laughed. "You get a lot of lovely packages for me Leenie, why call me about this one?"

"Because this one happens to be from one Ms. Abigail Reese. I can always put it in your pick up pile for the end of the month if—"

"Don't you dare!" I practically screamed as I almost jumped out of the makeup chair.

Rhonda, the makeup artist working on me, gave me a stern look. I mouthed 'sorry' as I sat back down.

"Can you bring it to the studio? If not, I'll swing by on my lunch break. It'll be a dash, but I can make it."

"I won't torture you and make you wait. I'll bring it to your trailer in about an hour." Arlene could tell how excited I was about the package from Abigail. I'm sure she was tickled pink over the entire situation. "I know you've been waiting for this."

"Thank you." I blew a kiss into the phone.

I wasn't able to get back to my trailer until lunch break. I begged off grabbing a bite with some cast mates and practically sprinted back to my trailer. Turning the corner heading for the corral, I stopped dead in my tracks. I took a double take and was shocked to see Bianca Monroe talking to Andie the showrunner. I couldn't fathom why she was talking to Bianca, but I knew it couldn't be good, especially not for me. The last thing I needed right now was that kind of poison walking back into my life.

I made a mental note to tell Arlene and see if she could find out what was going on. If it was bad I knew she would always go to bat for me, and bring out the barracuda fangs if she needed to. Shaking the feeling off, I put it out of my mind. I had a gift waiting for me. and I couldn't wait to open it.

I couldn't miss the box sitting on my little coffee table when I walked in. There was a note on the top of the box, left by Arlene. *'Don't forget to tell me what's inside!'* I sat down and carefully opened the box. I felt a sense of joy when I saw that Abigail had left me a note. *'Showing you a little of mine now. I hope you like what you see. - Abi'* I sat back on the couch and smiled as her scent lingered on the note. I wished she was here in Canada with me. There was so much more I wanted to learn about her.

I grabbed a bottle of water and my chicken caesar salad
from my mini-fridge before opening anything else. Making
myself comfortable I moved the tissue paper aside and
pulled out the poem. Touching the daisy on the top I
made a mental note that Abigail was crafty, and from
reading the poem, she had respect for, and a strong pull to
nature. I traced the flower with my index finger one last
time before setting it aside to read the next piece.

I carefully looked over the next piece. I loved the inge-
nuity of the ribbon closure and wondered if she had a craft
drawer somewhere in her apartment. I'd have to take a
look when I went to see her. My pulse raced at the
thought of seeing Abigail again, touching her, hearing her
laugh, curling a braid between my fingers. Shaking my
head I came back to the present so I could read the first
short story.

From the second sentence I was enveloped in her
words, in the world she had created. By the end I was
wiping away a few tears. I put it down and took a big swig
of water. I wanted to read the other one, but I needed to
finish my lunch and meditate before I returned to set. I
put the story and the poem back in the box and sent a
thank you text to Abigail as I finished my lunch.

For once I was glad that the weather had stalled film-

ing. It meant I had an early night and could call Abigail
even earlier.

Abigail picked up quickly. "Hello?"

"Hello my lovely."

"You're done early tonight."

I could hear her getting comfortable on what I
assumed was the couch. "Aye, the director had to cut the
day short due to a location glitch. Hopefully we'll be able
to use it in the morning."

"But of course you can't tell me where it was."

I chuckled. "Exactly, but I can tell you it involved
water and maybe a stunt or two."

"Ooh, I'm intrigued."

"Maybe you should start watching the show then." I
mused. For some reason I really wanted her to watch the
show. At least a couple of episodes.

Abigail ignored my comment. "Do you do your own
stunts?"

"I do what the studio will allow me to do. But some
stunts, they outright refuse to even let me try."

"Well, speaking from a totally selfish perspective I'm
glad they keep you on a tight leash."

"Oh, so you want me tied with a leash do you?" I
chuckled, letting my Irish brogue ooze from every word.

"Oh my god no! That's not what I meant!" she gave a
nervous laugh.

Even over the phone I knew just how to fluster Abigail,
and probably make her blush. I also hoped I was making
her picture me in naughty positions. Or even better letting
me put her in naughty positions. I gave myself a slap on
the wrist. We were not there yet.

"So something involving water, are you a good swimmer?"

I smiled knowing I had flustered her in the best way possible which is why she had changed the subject. I would let her off the hook for now. "Yes, I swim very well. I was actually on my secondary school swim team for two years, until I got bored with it."

"So, not a team player?" she chided.

"Oh I was, but I was more into girls and football, or what you call soccer, by the end of second year. What about you? Are you a swimmer?"

I heard Abigail take a sip of something. At this hour I was guessing it was tea. "Very much so, always been a water baby. I'm a regular mermaid."

"Ah, so I wouldn't have to worry about you falling overboard and not being able to swim."

"Are we on a boat or cruise ship?"

I silently cursed at myself for jumping the gun, but had I really? I thought for a moment before I answered her. "Not sure yet, either I guess."

"Well, as long as I don't hit my head on the way down. I'll be fine."

"Good to know." And now I couldn't stop thinking about taking Abigail on a cruise, maybe around next Christmas to someplace warm and tropical. The thought took me off guard since I hadn't even seen her since our first encounter and here I was thinking about taking her on a trip. I absentmindedly pulled at my lower lip but stopped myself after a minute.

"Where did you go?" Abigail asked. "I feel like you are further away than Toronto,"

"Sorry, I was just thinking about you in the water."

"I almost drowned once."

That got my attention. "What? How?" I was no longer relaxed on my couch.

"It happened a long time ago. I was maybe seven. I was coming out of the water and a wave got me from behind, knocked me on my ass and took me back out with it."

"Oh my god! That must have been terrible."

Abigail let out a small sigh. "Not really, Oddly enough I was really calm and I held my breath until the wave spit me rightside up. The scariest part was being so far from where my parents had been. I lost my bearings and it took me a while to walk all the way back to them."

"They didn't come looking for you?" I was confused by this."

Abigail sighed into the phone, this time it was much deeper and there was something behind it. Sorrow, if I were to take a guess. "I learned at a very early age that I couldn't rely on my parents, and that I needed to learn to rely on myself."

"Well, now you can rely on me too. I'll always have your back, waves be damned." And I truly meant what I told her.

Abigail's voice caught in her throat for a moment. I knew she believed me. "Thank you."

Nothing else needed to be said.

~ ABIGAIL ~

The last month and a half went by quickly. I wasn't sure which made me happier, the knowledge that my kids were beginning to grasp Chaucer or that I would be seeing Liam in less than twenty-four hours. Endless hours of daily phone calls, intimate emails, and several facetimes could not make up for the flesh and blood person standing in front of me.

Liam had teased me about not sharing his opinion of my writing until he saw me in person. I was dying to know his thoughts, but on the upside, it did give us a lot of time to just talk and get to know each other. But I still wasn't brave enough to divulge the full truth to Liam. And I knew the longer I waited the worse it would be.

No homework would be assigned this weekend. It was the last period of the day and I sat at my desk grading the pop-quiz I had just given while my students were working on a poem assignment. As I handed them back, I made one last announcement. "Don't forget auditions for the spring play are today after school. There will be more on

Monday if you can't make it today, but are interested in trying out. I know some of you are disappointed we aren't doing a musical. But with our musical director out on maternity leave, it just isn't possible. But *Merry Widows, Merry Brides* is a very funny play that I'm sure you'll enjoy being a part of."

The bell rang, and even though I had more to say, it was Friday, and as soon as the chime of that bell went off, my students' ears shut down as well as their brains. Their only thoughts were of the weekend out in the weather that was finally beginning to consistently stay warm and sunny. "Have a good weekend," I shouted as they filed out the door. I couldn't get the smile off my face as I headed to the auditorium for the auditions. There was already a group of drama students gathering. Margot, who was acting as my assistant director, was there handing out sides.

"Thank you all for coming. Margot will call you in one at a time to audition. Cast list will be posted Tuesday morning. Good luck to you all." With that I entered the auditorium and got myself set up to hear the same couple of monologues and scenes over and over for the next two hours. I looked at my phone one last time before they began.

~ LIAM ~

It was between takes and the shooting day was almost done. I only had one last scene to shoot for the day and then I would be heading to the airport to fly out to Connecticut. My brain was in a battle between trying to stay in the moment of the scenes and thinking about Abigail and what I would or wouldn't do to her this weekend.

"Oh man, I'm in trouble." I turned to my co-star and friend, Ted Rendfelt. He played the popular character Flint on the show. "Teddy, what am I going to do?"

"What's up man? Worried about your plans for the weekend? You can always come with me and Connie. We're heading to Montreal. Do a little dining, a little wining. You know, straight up R&R."

"That sounds lovely, but I'm going down to Connecticut."

Ted whistled. "Really, back to see that woman you were telling me about. Amy, no, Annie?"

"Abi, yeah. God, I must be crazy to think about starting something."

"Woah! When you mean start something, are you talking like a nice booty call whenever you have the time or an itch to scratch? Or are you talking about starting something, something?"

"No man, I'm talking about something, something. I'm talking it's absolutely bonkers how immediately I was attracted to this lass and on such a deeper level than just the physical, and man is she gorgeous!"

"No offense, but I saw a picture of the two of you and she seems, let's just say she is not the average woman you've dated in the past."

"Why? Because she isn't some stick model?" I practically growled.

"Hey man! Don't get mad. I'm just stating the obvious."

I sighed. "Sorry, I didn't mean to bite your head off. I know, I know she isn't the usual type of woman I flash on the red carpet. But to be honest it's the type I've liked all along and didn't allow myself to be with after my career took off. I'm embarrassed to admit I listened to the wrong people, but now I don't care what people say or think. I care about what I want. I'm getting thoughts and feelings I haven't had since, since—"

"Since Miss Bianca Monroe."

"Right." I nodded.

"Yup, you're in trouble." Ted patted my arm. "Look Liam, if you really are into this Abi woman then I say go for it. Take it one day at a time and just enjoy it. You deserve some happiness."

I smiled. "I do, don't I?"

"It's been long enough man. It's time. Oh wait, is she a fan of the show? She's not like some stalker in disguise or something?"

I chuckled. "That's the best part mate. She doesn't even watch the show. She's more of a reader, and a theatre goer than a sci-fi fantasy gal."

"Then I say, have a great weekend." He got up out of his chair. "But for now, keep your head in the game man. I don't want to have to do take after take because your big brain isn't working."

I laughed. "Not a problem, I'm a man on a mission."

~ ABIGAIL ~

The auditions went well. There were some good choices in the group that came through. But Margot and I promised each other not to have anyone set in mind until we saw all the auditions. We had one more day on Monday before we would make our decisions. "So Margot. Are you getting a taste for directing?"

Margot laughed. "I'm not sure about that, but I do like the casting part."

"I'm going to ask you one last time. Are you sure you don't want to audition yourself? I can direct by myself if you want to throw your hat in the ring."

Margot shook her head. "No, if we were doing a musical, I'd be all about it, but I was in the fall play. Being your assistant gives me something new to try."

"Alright, as long as you're sure. Then I'll see you Monday in class, and after school for the rest of the auditions. Have a great weekend, Margot."

"You too Miss Reese. Any big plans?" Margot asked with a sly smile on her face.

"Who knows?" I gave her a wink. "See you Monday."

I gave Margot a final wave and headed for the grocery store. I still needed to get things for my special Saturday dinner. I had gone back and forth in my mind what exactly I wanted to make. At this point the only thing I was sure of was that I wanted to make some charlotte russe for dessert, and a nice garden salad.

Over the years, I had managed to have a very nice window box garden that stretched across the three windows of my living room. I had a small balcony on my fifth story apartment so I had access to them from both sides. I had been able to grow some lovely herbs as well as some cherry tomatoes, some carrots, and some kale. With the help of a small hothouse that the landlord had looked the other way on. It took up half my balcony but it was worth it. I had fresh vegetables at my disposal almost year round now. I was thankful to my father for teaching me how to have a green thumb. It paid off well in the winter months.

I picked up some freshly made french bread. Maybe I would go Italian and make some homemade garlic bread. But we had gone to an Italian restaurant on their first date.

I let out a laugh. I still couldn't believe what I just had been thinking about, our *'first date'*. I cleared my head and wandered through the meat and seafood sections to see if anything jumped out at me. Maybe a beef wellington? Or shrimp and grits? Lobster tails and scallops? Or maybe some juicy crab legs with drawn butter? I imagined watching Liam suck the meat from deep inside the leg of a crab. Maybe see a single drip of butter that he licked up with his tongue. Yes, that was it. The thought made me stumble a bit as my knees slightly buckled underneath me. Crab legs it would be, and the garlic bread and salad would go perfectly with them. I picked up several pounds of snow crab legs and then headed home.

I could feel my phone vibrating in my pocket as I unlocked my front door. I quickly put my bags on the kitchen island and pulled my phone out to answer it. "Hello?" I practically shouted.

"Hello lovely."

I smiled when I heard Liam's voice. "I was just thinking about you."

"Oh really? What were you thinking?" Liam asked. There was mischief in his tone. I could only imagine what thoughts were going through his mind at the moment. I doubted they were all sweet and fuzzy.

"I'm not sure if I should tell you." I laughed.

"Well, if you don't want to share, I'll just leave it to my imagination." Liam gave a husky laugh.

I bit my lip, wondering what wonderful things his imagination could lead to. I snapped myself out of it. "So, have you left for the airport yet?"

"Actually that's what I'm calling about. There has been a change in plans."

My heart sank a little, but I tried not to sound disappointed. I was worried at some point he would cancel. Either because his schedule changed, or he just changed his mind. It would make sense if he was changing his mind. The trip was a little much for only the weekend which didn't even come to two full days together with all the travel time. "Okay, did your work schedule change or something?

"As a matter of fact it did."

"That's okay, I understand." I took a deep breath, and smiled, so I wouldn't sound upset.

I heard a chuckle on the other end of the phone that grew until it was a full on loud belly laugh. "I'm sorry I couldn't resist teasing you a little. You might be okay with me canceling, but I wouldn't be. We finished early so I was able to catch an earlier flight and I'm already at the hotel. Care to go for dinner? I'm starving."

"Oh!" I laughed in relief. "That's not what I was expecting you to hear. But yes, I would love to go to dinner with you."

"I can pick you up in say half an hour?"

"That sounds perfect." I did a mini happy dance in my kitchen.

"Alright, I just need your address and I'll see you in thirty minutes."

I gave him my address and hung up. I couldn't stop smiling as I put the rest of the groceries away and tidied up my apartment a little. Even though I wasn't expecting him to see my place until tomorrow, I had already started the cleaning process so there wasn't much left to do. Once that was done, I realized I only had fifteen minutes left to get ready.

I jumped in the shower for a quick wash down. Seven minutes later I was out of the shower and fully lotioned. I could thank years of being a summer camp counselor for my ability to take quick showers. Standing in front of my closet, I debated on what to wear. I decided to go with something casual, but pretty. It was a little chilly for a sundress and I didn't know where he wanted to take me, so I decided on a flowy green skirt that went down to just below my knees. It kind of resembled a peasant skirt but a little more classy because of the material used and the lace trim on the bottom. For the top I chose a simple long sleeve, black v-neck. It showed off my cleavage quite well.

I always got a look or two when I wore it. It was also great because it showed off the necklace I wanted to wear. It was a wonderful gift from Tess, it was a beautiful Celtic knot design in rose gold. I was putting on my lipstick when the door buzzer went off. I went into the living room and hit the intercom button. "Hello?"

"It's me, can I come up?"

I buzzed him in. and ran to my bathroom to spritz some perfume on. A few minutes later there was a knock at my door. I opened it to see a smiling Liam with a small bouquet of flowers. "Hello my lovely." He handed me the flowers.

I inhaled deeply and smiled. "You're going to spoil me if you keep giving me flowers."

~ LIAM ~

I entered Abigail's apartment, shutting the door behind me. "Beautiful ladies deserve beautiful flowers."

Abigail gave me a quick kiss on the lips. "Thank you so much. I'll just go put these in water. Come in, make yourself comfortable." Abigail went to the kitchen.

I watched as she pulled down a vase from the top of the fridge and some scissors from a drawer. She ran the stems under the water and cut them on a diagonal. "Do you always cut your flowers like that?"

She nodded, "Yes, my father taught me how to do it this way."

I came up behind her as she began arranging them in the vase, I wrapped my arms around her waist and began kissing her neck. She had her braids up so it was easy access. I heard her gasp and she almost dropped the vase when I hit a certain spot. I made a mental note of it.

"Hi," I whispered between kisses. "I didn't realize how much I missed you until you opened the door." I gripped her hips and gently bit her shoulder before going back to kissing it. I was feeling bold so I snaked my hand over her shoulder and down her v-neck. I caressed her breast over her bra. My height advantage was coming in handy.

Abigail whispered "I missed you too."

I turned her around and took her face in my hands. I dropped little kisses over her eyes and her forehead, and down her cheeks. Her breathing changed slightly with every kiss."I, I thought you were starving."

I looked into her amber eyes, licked my lips and winked. "I am." I planted a kiss on her lips, soft at first but then with more pressure, demanding entrance. She opened her mouth to me, letting our tongues entwine. I pressed my entire body against Abigail so she could feel just how happy I was to see her.

To my pleasant surprise Abigail grabbed my ass, drawing me even closer. I groaned as I grinded up against her. I moved her v-neck over exposing her bra. Moving it aside, I peppered her breasts with tiny butterfly kisses.

Abigail arched her back wanting more. "Couch," she whispered as she bit my ear.

I took her hand and led her to the couch. I sat her down and began kissing her again. She drew me down on top of her. I stopped for a moment sitting us up so I could take her shirt off. I kissed her neck as I unhooked her bra. My hands immediately went to her small yet supple breast, cupping them fully. For a plus size woman she had smaller breasts than most would assume, but they were perfect for me. I kneaded them in my hand as I kissed and licked at her neck.

Abigail tried to get my shirt off. Finally I took it off for her. She ran her hands along my six pack. She gently ran her fingernails over each muscle before she began kissing it.I let her for a moment but then pulled her face up to mine and began kissing her again, biting her lower lip before drawing her tongue into my mouth so I could suck on it, gently moving her further down on the couch. I started kissing down her body, stopping at her breasts.

This is where I took my time, kissing and licking at each nipple before taking one in my mouth and gently sucking on it and then moving to the other, loving the sounds coming from Abigail as my tongue swirled around each hard bud. I could tell she was going to be loud when I finally made her come. The thought made me harder than I already was. I bit her nipple making her cry out, arching her back even more. Her cries only spurred me on.

~ ABIGAIL ~

Fuck! I was getting so wet, but I wasn't sure if I wanted to sleep with him just yet. But he felt so good on top of me and I could feel that he was rock hard. I wanted him inside me so badly. But this was still so new. Was it too soon?

Liam could feel something was off. My thoughts betrayed my body. "Abi, are you alright? Do you want me to stop?"

I took a moment to catch my breath. "No, I mean yes, I mean, you feel so good, but I don't know."

I said this knowing how Liam would react. We had talked every day since he had sent me the photographs. We had shared a lot. I knew Liam had been raised with a very respectful father, a loving mother and two sisters. He knew that the only yes was a yes. Maybe, or I don't know, meant no. He immediately stopped and sat up.

"Talk to me, what's going on?" He wrapped a blanket that was on the couch over my shoulders so I could cover up. He ran his hand through his hair, trying to slow his breath as he calmed himself.

"Can I ask you something and I need you to be completely honest with me?" I chewed the corner of my lip.

"Of course."

"Am I just a booty call for you? Am I your chance at a fat girl conquest?" The words rushed out of my mouth and hung in the air.

Liam looked stunned by my question. "Where on earth was that coming from? Abi, I would never treat you like that. Nor do I even think of you like that."

"How do you think of me?" I was almost afraid to ask, but since I had already opened the box I might as well see what was inside.

Liam took my hand and kissed it. "I think of you as a lovely woman who I am sharing what I hope will be a very long and very loving relationship with. I think of you as the person I need and deserve in my life. I know this has all been going so fast but it also feels so right. Don't fight it. I'm not."

I tried not to cry at his words. He made me feel so beautiful and so desirable, both in his actions and words. It had been a very long time since anyone had made me feel like that. I grabbed his face and kissed him. "You are so incredibly special to me." I kissed him again drawing him down on top of me, wrapping my legs around his waist.

We kissed for a while until Liam pulled back. "Abi, not that I don't love making out with you, but if we don't stop soon, I'm going to want to taste you, and then I'll want -" He paused for a moment as he raised his eyebrow. "More."

I smiled and gave him one last kiss. "Okay, then we should stop. I'm not quite ready for more yet. I want more, but not yet. Is that okay?"

Liam pulled me up, so we were both in a sitting position. "That's perfectly fine, my lovely." He bent down to pick up his shirt and put it back on. "But we still have a problem."

I just watched him cover up his beautiful body. "And that is?"

"I'm still starving."

I laughed. "Let's order in. How do you feel about Thai food?"

"Sounds perfect." He smiled as he tucked his shirt into his pants.

We ordered food and decided to eat in the living room while watching some shows on DTV. When dinner was done, I made us ice cream sundaes. I had caramel ice cream. He had chocolate. I scooped a dollop of ice cream and made sure there was some whipped cream and caramel on it. I held it up to Liam's lips. "Taste?" Liam opened his mouth for me. I gently put the spoonful of ice cream goodness in his mouth. He closed his eyes as he closed his mouth around the spoon. I pulled it out slowly. "Mmm, that tastes good."

"Want some more?"

"I'll take another spoonful." Liam smiled.

I put a spoonful in my mouth and then kissed Liam, sharing the ice cream with him. He deepened the kiss, grabbing my shoulder, almost massaging it. He groaned as he pulled away. "You are killing me, woman."

"Sorry, I don't mean to. I just like kissing you." I nuzzled his nose with mine.

"I know the feeling." We made out some more, letting the ice cream melt in the bowls as a design show droned on in the background. We eventually broke apart. "I should get going. It's late."

"You could stay." I traced his jaw line down to his lips.

Liam smiled. "I would love to, but I don't know if I can trust myself. You are quite irresistible, you know."

He was right. I had said I wanted to wait and now I was teasing him. It wasn't fair and I needed to check myself. "How about we go to the farmers market tomorrow? Or maybe the movies before I cook you dinner?"

"Either one is fine with me. Or we can do both if we start early enough." Liam got up and tucked his shirt inside his pants. I had pulled it out again, so I could caress his magnificent torso. "I can pick you up at ten?"

"Ten, I like ten. That works for me." I wrapped my hands around his waist and kissed him. Soft kisses. He kissed me back just as softly.

"I'm going to leave now. Because I'm a minute away from taking you to your bedroom," Liam stated between kisses.

I sighed as he pulled away. "Alright, go get some rest, and I'll see you at ten sharp." I gave him one last kiss and walked him to the door.

~ LIAM ~

The next morning I was true to my word, ten am sharp I buzzed for entrance to Abigail's apartment building. She buzzed me in but not before talking into the intercom.

"Door is unlocked, just come on in," she said into the buzzer.

I shook my head as I headed up. What if it wasn't me who she had buzzed in? She needed to be more careful. I couldn't have her leaving her door unlocked for anyone to stroll in. But the moment I entered her apartment and saw her, my scolding flew right out of my head. I found her by the hall mirror pulling her hair up into a ponytail.

"I really do love your braids." I twirled a couple between my hands as I gave her a kiss. "Good morning, my lovely. How did you sleep?"

"Oh, nice sunglasses." She mentioned as she looked me up and down." I slept very well, how about you?"

"Sweet, sweet dreams." I smiled. I clapped my hands

together. "Come, let's start our day, shall we?"I pulled a baseball cap out of my back pocket.

Abigail looked at me. I just shrugged and adjusted my cap. She smiled.

"I get it." She grabbed her purse and my hand. "Come on."

We stopped for coffee at a little shop around the corner from her apartment before walking the five blocks to the market in the park. Abigail was cheerful, swinging my arm as we walked. "Happy?" I asked.

She nodded, a wide grin making her face beam. "It's the first market of the season. It means that spring has officially sprung." Her joy was contagious.

We picked up some fresh flowers and some pretzels. Then we grabbed some apricots and raw honey as well as some heavy cream from a dairy farmer and some of his coffee milk. Abigail led me along and I happily followed. "You know this market well. Look at you with your cloth bags, and one cold bag already packed with ice. I love a well prepared woman." I gave her hand a squeeze.

We stopped at a booth that had some wonderful home-made essential oils. Abigail picked up some honeysuckle and I got myself some patchouli as well as some sandal-wood. "I should have known that you would like essential oils." The more I learned about Abigail the more I liked her.

As Abigail was paying, I saw a young woman, a teenager really, staring at us out of the corner of my eye. I grabbed Abigail's hand and started moving along to some other booths. I sighed as I saw that the girl was following us. I pulled Abigail a little closer. She stopped at another booth to look at some used books. That's when the young lady following us approached me.

"Excuse me, are you Liam Caffney?"

Abigail looked up from the books she was looking at. I patted her hand signaling her that everything was fine. I put on one of my winning smiles. "Yes, I am."

The girl smiled and started gushing immediately. "Oh my god I thought it was you! What are you doing here?! I love you on the show! I really hope Lochlan and Beatrice end up together. Isla isn't good enough for you. I mean Lochlan. Oh my god! I can't believe I'm standing in front of you right now! Can you give me any hints for next season?"

"Woah there, now why don't we start with your name?"

"Oh yes! Sorry," she giggled. "My name is Nina, I'm Nina. I'm a huge fan! Probably one of your biggest. I even run a fan site about the show. It's called 'Lochlan of Ever-Morph'. Have you seen it? You probably haven't, but that's okay. Can I get a picture with you? I can't wait to post this." Nina spoke a mile a minute.

More people started to notice what was happening. This Nina girl seemed to be getting louder and louder the more she talked. And she seemed to have quite a lot to say. She had to be around fifteen, or sixteen and she had the teen squeal down pat.

Abigail saw the other people taking note and her body language as well as her facial expression changed. It was like she was nervous, anxious almost. I couldn't blame her. I knew she had never experienced something like this. And this was just a mild little moment. I worried how she would feel at something larger.

I took a quick scan of the area. There was no security here. I'm sure there had to be at least one police officer strolling around somewhere but there were none in sight. We were in an open park.

I looked at Liam, he seemed cool as a cucumber. But what if more people came? I could see a curious crowd of onlookers start to form. They were at a distance , but how long would it stay like that? This Nina girl seemed to be shrieking. At least that's what it sounded like to me. This was a perfect example of why I didn't want to be associated with fans. It was because of shrieking girls like this, or the ones who didn't know the difference between the character and the actor. People like that were thought of as the rule, not the exception. "Liam?"

Liam turned slightly and saw the look on my face. He pulled me close to him, taking my hand and gave it a reassuring squeeze. He didn't let go. "Nina, this is my girl Abi. I'm sure she would be happy to take the picture you requested. Right, Abi?" He squeezed my hand again.

I took a deep breath and smiled. I could totally handle this. "Yes, of course. I take it you are a fan of *EverMorphs*?"

I tried to act like I was having trouble remembering the name of the show.

Nina looked at me like I had three heads, but she handed me her phone anyway to take the picture. I moved away from Liam as Nina moved closer so that I could get a good shot.

I raised my eyebrow as this teenager leaned into Liam's chest, and wrapped an arm around his waist "Okay, smile." I snapped a picture.

"Take another one, will you Abi please?" Liam put both of his arms around Nina in a side hug. She looked like she was in heaven.

I could tell this picture would be blown up, framed, and hung relatively close to Nina's bed. That's what I would have done at her age. I took two more photos and then handed Nina her phone back. "It was very nice to meet you, Nina. I hope you like the pictures I took."

Nina looked at the photos on her phone and grinned ear to ear. "They are perfect, thank you so much."

"Anytime." I nodded and then turned back to the owner of the booth to pay for the books she had set aside for me. I wanted to give Liam a moment to say goodbye to Nina in private.

Liam was signing the hat Nina had on when she looked over at me. "Wait, you said she was your girl? The woman who took the picture for me, is she your new girlfriend?"

Liam looked over at Abigail and winked. He turned back to Nina with a big smile on his face. "Well yes, yes she is. And as my biggest fan you are officially the first person to know. But can you keep it a secret? Just for a little while?"

Nina looked me up and down several times, before

giving a slight nod and smile. She seemed to approve. "Of course I can."

"Oh, thank you darlin'. Now we've got to be going, but it was very nice meeting you, Nina." Liam took my hand as I moved towards them, putting the books in the bag he was holding.

"Bye!" Nina waved as we walked away. She immediately got on her phone. We could hear her as she walked away "OMG Stacy! You'll never guess who I just met!"

Liam put his arm around me as we continued walking away.

I turned to Liam "So, I'm your girl, am I? You know she took pictures of us walking away."

"Ay, I'm aware. I'm also sure she won't keep seeing us together a secret." He stopped her for a moment, taking both of my hands in his. "I'm sorry. I know we haven't really talked about what we are. If there even is an 'us' in that way. But that's how I think of you. I've felt like that since I stepped off the plane. You're my girl and it's time people knew it."

I kissed him and stroked his cheek. "I like being 'your girl'." I kissed him again.

The way Liam looked into my eyes and the beating of his heart, I knew how he felt. Because I was feeling the same. We were both opening up. Liam kissed me, deeply and held me close. And I knew he didn't care who saw us. I began to moan softly as I felt like I was melting into him. He finally had to pull away. "We should head back to your apartment, but take the long way back."

"You don't want to see the rest of the market?"

Liam shook his head. "I can guess that Nina called all of her friends and they will soon descend upon this lovely market. I'd rather not be here for that, and I can guarantee neither do you."

I nodded in agreement. I followed Liam's lead as he made an eight block loop back to my apartment. Once inside I put our purchases away. "Are you still up for a movie?" I wasn't sure if he wanted to stay hidden after the encounter with Nina.

"I'd love to sit in a dark theater with you Abi." Liam wrapped his arms around me as he leaned down giving me a slow lingering kiss. I could have stayed like that forever, but we had plans.

"You want to drive?" I asked as I dangled my car keys.

Liam grabbed them from me as we headed out the door. He drove as I gave him direction. The entire ride he kept his hand on my thigh.

I had picked a theatre that showed old movies. It was a sure way I wouldn't run into any of my students at the theater. "How old school do you want to go?" I asked as Liam parked the car.

"What do you mean?"

"Well, we can go back to the fifties and watch *Singin' in the Rain*. But that's a musical, so if you don't like them we should skip it. We can go back to the seventies and watch *Jaws*. Or we could go way way back and see *The Death Kiss*. A mystery from the thirties."

"Hmm, they all sound interesting. Although I haven't seen many musicals in my lifetime. So I'm not sure how much I'll like it. What do you want to see?"

"It's your weekend. You choose." I smiled.

"Okay, then let's go with *Jaws*."

I took his hand and led him into the theater. "*Jaws* it is."

~ LIAM ~

"Come on, tell me you wouldn't scream like that if a great white was trying to eat you." I argued.

"I'm sorry, I love the movie, but I don't think the scream was realistic. I never thought it was," Abigail stated as she opened her apartment door. "Make yourself at home. I need to start dinner. Can I get you something to drink?"

"Anything you have is fine." I made myself comfortable on the couch.

"Do you prefer alcoholic or non-alcoholic?" Abigail called from the kitchen.

"Let's go with non-alcoholic drinks for now. I like to drink with dinner."

"Good point," Abigail said as she came into the living room with a glass of ice tea. She even had a lemon wedge on the edge of the glass.

I took the glass and put it down on the coffee table. I pulled Abigail down on the couch and began kissing her. I slid my hands under her shirt and caressed her back for a while before trying to undo her bra. I was having trouble and it made Abigail laugh.

"I'm taking this as a sign we should stop."

I nuzzled her neck giving it little kisses and gentle bites as I went. It made Abigail sigh. Her breathing was becoming raspy. "Are you sure you want me to stop?" I asked as I put her hand on my cock that was beginning to get hard. She gave it a gentle squeeze and began rubbing it through my jeans.I groaned, squeezing her shoulder. My lips met hers, Each of us opening our mouths to the other. Tongues entangled, both breathing heavier.

A buzzer went off in the kitchen. Abigail sighed as she slowly pulled away. "The water is ready for the crab."

"No, stay with me." I kissed her again.

Abigail laughed. "There will be plenty of time for this later."

I raised an eyebrow. "Is that a promise?"

Abigail winked as she headed to the kitchen. "We'll see."

I took a long sip of ice tea once I put the crab legs in. Liam was making me very hot, and it was becoming hard to resist him. But if I was honest with myself, I really didn't want to. I took another sip, trying to refocus myself on the task at hand. I made the garlic bread, using freshly chopped garlic, put it in foil and set it aside. It wasn't time to go into the oven yet.

Next I started on the salad, but I needed tomato. "Liam, can you grab some tomatoes from the balcony for me?" I waited for an answer, but didn't get one. "Liam?" I walked into the living room. Liam was asleep curled under the blanket I kept on the couch. Beatrice was curled up on his hip. I watched him for a minute and smiled.

A runaway curl had fallen on his face. I gently tucked it behind his ear and kissed his forehead. "What am I going to do with you? You are capturing my heart minute by minute," I whispered. I kissed his forehead again and headed to the balcony to grab some tomatoes.

~ LIAM ~

I opened my eyes as Abigail walked away. "I know the feeling," I whispered, as I closed my eyes again, and fell back to sleep. It wasn't long before the smells from the kitchen tickled my nose and wandered into my dreams, waking me up. I looked down to see a very pretty cat staring at me. I gave it a scratch under the chin before scooping it up in my arms. "Hello there little one."

I noticed a copy of *The Canterbury Tales* on the little shelf under Abigail's coffee table. I began to look through it as one of the cats made itself comfortable on my lap. I think it was Cassiopeia, since it was the girl. I was sure Dipper was the boy.

"She must really like you. I can hear her purring from here."

I looked up to see Abigail leaning in the door frame. She had an apron on and the cutest smile on her face. "That's one of my favorites. But I think you know that already." She said.

"Your help has been invaluable. It would have stayed a

jumbled mess without you. Is your class still on *The Pardon-er's Tale?*" The cat jumped off my lap. And walked over to its mother winding its body around Abigail's legs.

"We finished that tale. We're on *The Wife of Bath*. My seniors are having a really hard time with it. I'm trying to make it easier for them but it's a challenge. Hey, dinner is ready."

I put the book down and followed her into the dining room. "I'm starving. What did you—" I stopped when I saw the table setting. Abigail had put the flowers from the market in a vase in the center, and had cut them nice and low so that we could see each other across the table. She had also set out some candles and dimmed the lights. Fancy wine glasses were filled with what I could only imagine was our favorite wine that we had discussed on our very first date.

It was obvious she had put out the good china as well, salad bowls included. I whistled. "Wow, this looks amazing! Did you do all of this while I was sleeping?"

Abigail nodded as she set the still warm garlic bread on the table. "I even pre-cracked the crab."

"Careful Abi, you're spoiling me. I might get used to this." I chuckled.

Abigail kissed my cheek before sitting down. "Good! Now let's dig in."

I took a piece of my pre-cracked grab and dipped it in the lemon and butter sauce in the little dipping carafe and popped it in my mouth. "Mmm, this is amazing!" I quickly took another bite. "So, so good. You may have missed your calling. I see a chef in you." It had been a long time since anyone had made me a home cooked meal, let alone one that tasted this good.

"So tell me, why were you reading *The Pardoner's Tale*? It isn't your average light reading." Abigail licked some butter from her finger tip.

I put my fork down. "Okay, so what I am about to say you cannot tell anyone. I can trust you right?"

"Of course."

I couldn't believe I was about to break my confidentiality clause, but I hadn't felt this safe around anyone besides Arlene in years. It felt right."I'm going to be shooting a new television series and it's based on *The Canterbury Tales*. I'll be playing the Pardoner in this new updated sci-fi version."

"You're leaving your current show?" Abigail practically shouted.

I looked at her for a moment. It wasn't the response I was expecting. "No, not at all. This is just a little project between seasons. A limited series. I have no intention of leaving EverMorphs anytime soon."

"Oh, okay." Abigail tried to play it off cool.

But it wasn't working. Something was off. For a split second I worried I had just confided something to a *'fan'* and not the woman I was falling for. I ignored the warning voice in my head. That was not the type of person Abigail was. So I continued. "But there is more."

"Am I going to like it?" Abigail wiped her mouth and sat up a little straighter. She looked like she was stealing herself for some bad news.

I gave her a coy little smirk. "I hope so."

"Don't keep me in suspense. Tell me."

I took a sip of wine to draw out the suspense.

"Don't make me pout Liam. You wouldn't like me when I pout." Abigail stuck her lower lip out.

I laughed. "You look hot even when you pout. Especially that bottom lip of yours, it's just begging to be bit."

Abigail licked her lips and then stuck out her bottom one a little more. "Liam, tell me."

"Okay, sorry. What I wanted to tell you was that it is filming for two months about an hour north of here."

"Wait, what?" A wide smile popped up on Abigail's face. "I need you to say it again. Just to be sure I heard you correctly."

"I will be only one hour away from you for two months. I have two months of filming left in Toronto and then two weeks off and then filming. Just sixty short minutes away."

"So I get you almost all summer?" Abigail was trying to contain her excitement.

I nodded. "But I do have some contest thing I have to participate in somewhere in there. The winner hasn't been picked yet so I don't know where I'll be flying. So, I'll be gone for a couple of days for that. The show is sponsoring it. They are hoping it will help the arts in public schools."

Abigail nodded. "They need it. They are always the first programs cut, but the ones most needed."

This was going better than I thought so I decided to press my luck. "I was hoping maybe I could just stay here with you on my days off?"

Abigail nodded as she got up from her seat and hugged me. "I would really really love that."

We talked about all the things we could do over the summer. I don't think I had ever looked more forward to a break from The EverMorphs than now.

Dinner had been wonderful, but I couldn't take it anymore. I took a deep breath and just dived in. I had to know. "So you promised to tell me what you thought about what I sent you to read."

Liam looked at me as he took a sip of this wine. He could see the apprehension on my face. I didn't share my writing very often, only with Tess really. I was genuinely worried he wouldn't like it. I knew I had talent, but a small shade of doubt always hung in the back of my mind. But I think all creatives had that feeling at one time or another.

Liam reached out for my hand and kissed it. "If I had only one day to capture the essence of your bloom, to memorize the soft ebb and flow of each delicate petal. To ingrain the luscious scent that emanates from your core into my senses for all time, it wouldn't be enough. For you are timeless, and sadly I am out of time."

I was shocked and wasn't sure how to respond. He was quoting from the poem I had sent him. I was speechless, all I could do was blush, an act he could not possibly see.

Liam gave my hand a squeeze. "Each story, each poem, were wonderful. They were all lovely, so full of life, passion, and dare I say pain. You really have a wonderful way of creating a world that anyone would long to be a part of, even in the tragic moments. I shed several tears when Anastasia lost her sweet babe."

A smile swept across my face as I let out the breath I had been holding. "I'm so glad you liked them."

Liam shook his head. "I didn't like them, I loved them. In fact, I passed one of your stories to Arlene, and she agreed with me. She asked if she could give it to an agent friend of hers, and I said yes."

"Why? What? Why did you do that? That was only for you!" I drained my wine glass and poured myself some more. What the hell was happening? I couldn't tell if I should be pissed or happy or both. I decided to go with pissed.

"Please don't be mad, they were just so wonderful." Liam looked me in the eye as he rubbed his thumb over the top of my hand.

I sighed. It was so hard to be pissed at him when he was just trying to help me. Even if it was help I didn't ask for. But I could tell there was more news from the face he was making. It was a face of hesitation. "I feel like there is more, so go ahead and tell me everything. But I reserve the right to be pissed." I squeezed his hand.

Liam took a deep breath and continued. "The good news is that her agent friend really liked it. She wants to meet you."

I was no longer pissed, I was elated, and also a little scared, and maybe a bit shocked. Liam had believed enough in me and my writing to pass it along to someone in the industry that could actually make it go somewhere. I had no words so I just leaned over and kissed him. "Thank you," I whispered as I clasped his face in my hands and looked into his eyes.

"I take it, you're not mad anymore?" Liam kissed me back.

I shook my head. "I am so far from mad."

"Then you should be hearing from Deana Cartwhile probably in the next week. I'll let Arlene know it's okay to give her your phone number."

I nodded. "I need to thank Arlene. I'll have to send her something. Does she like chocolate brownies?"

"They are one of her favorites."

"Okay, good. I'll make her some this week and send them with a thank you card."

Liam shook his head. "It's really not necessary."

"Maybe not for you, but it is for me, This is a really big deal for me and I want her to know I don't take it for granted. But for now, how do you feel about dessert in the living room?" I started to clear the table.

"That sounds wonderful but let me clean up love. You made such a lovely dinner, it's the least I can do."

I couldn't believe what he just said. A man that was willing to help in the kitchen. And I melted when he called me love or lovely, It was always said with tenderness. It made me feel special and made my heart skip a beat. "Thank you. I'll just get dessert started then."

Liam cleared the dishes, rinsed, and put them in the dishwasher. Then wiped down the table and moved the candles into the living room. While he did that I got out two dessert cups and filled it with charlotte russe. It was a dessert my mother had taught me how to make when I was about ten. It was made with either chocolate or vanilla cakes doused in either homemade vanilla whipped cream or homemade chocolate whipped cream. And chilled overnight. It was always best to do the opposite for the cake and whipped cream.

I had decided on vanilla cake and chocolate whipped cream. I dished it out and then made some amaretto coffees to go with it. I set up everything on a tray and brought it into the living room. I smiled when I saw what Liam had done. He had completely rearranged my living room and it was quite charming, and even a bit magical. I loved it.

Liam had made a little pillow nest for us using the lip of the couch as a place to lean pillows against. He had pulled pillows from the couch as well as from my bedroom. He had also set some blankets around and had turned the tv to a music station playing contemporary classics. I set the dessert tray on the coffee table.

"This nest is amazing, and I love the candles. Do you mind if I change before we eat? I want to be nice and cozy."

"Not at all love. Do whatever makes you comfortable."

I went into my bedroom, closing the door behind me. I put on a pair of sleep shorts and a sleep tank top. It was yellow with some light orange flowers on it, and although it wasn't silk, it was a shiny fabric that was cool and silky to the touch. I put my hair up in a loose ponytail with a braid or two flowing freely and walked back out into the living room.

Liam was already sitting in the nest sipping his coffee. Making himself comfortable, he had taken off his shoes and pulled his shirt out from his jeans. He whistled as I walked out. "Love, you look amazing."

I sat down next to him. "It's just some jammies." He made me feel so adored with the simplest of sentences.

"I like your jammies then." He put the blanket he had over his legs over mine as well. "May I?" He pointed to the dessert. He was such a gentleman, he hadn't touched them while I changed. He didn't want to start without me.

"Please." I handed him one of the cups and I took the other.

He took a bite. "Mmm, this is so good! I've never tasted something like this before."

"It's a family recipe. My mom taught me how to make it when I was around ten. It's one of my favorites. But I only make it for special occasions."

Liam cocked his head to the side. "So, I'm a special occasion?"

"Maybe." I smiled.

We ate in silence for a few minutes enjoying the music. Liam broke the silence. "Can I ask you something?"

"Anything."

"I know you aren't a fan of *The EverMorphs*. But are you a fan of anything?"

God, that was such a loaded question. I paused only for a moment, debating on telling him the truth, the whole truth and nothing but the truth. To confess all my sins and ask for his forgiveness. But instead I shook her head. "No, not anymore."

"What do you mean, not anymore?"

I sighed. My answer had left room for interpretation and it was obvious there was more behind the sentence. "I don't like being thought of as a fan. So I try not to like anything too much to be classified as one, or called one, or thought of as one, or treated like one." My voice became quicker and higher pitched with every word.

"Hey, it's okay. We don't have to talk about it." Liam put down his dessert and scooped me up in his arms. He just stayed like that until he could feel my body start to calm and relax itself. "I feel like there is a story there. But you don't have to tell me until you are ready. Just know that I am here."

I looked at Liam. I wanted to tell him what had happened to me all those years ago. What had made me start to hide what I was a fan of and confess just how much I loved his show and his talent. But again, I didn't dare. Instead I kissed him.

I kissed him with all the feelings I longed to tell him but was afraid to say. I ran my hands through his hair and down to the nape of his neck, letting them rest there so I could play with his curls as we continued kissing. I wanted more so I deepened the kiss. I leaned back, taking Liam with me. I loved the feeling of his weight on top of me. I squeezed his ass as I kissed his neck and ear and then back to his mouth. I ran my hands down his back, working my way under his shirt, feeling his warm skin against mine.

~ LIAM ~

I leaned us both up. I took my shirt off and then pulled her tank top off. I cupped her breasts and caressed them as he looked into her eyes. I relished rubbing the pads of my thumbs over her nipples making them harden under my touch. Abigail sucked in her breath as I did. I listened carefully to all the cues she gave me. Her nipples were a hot button. And I planned to explore them to their fullest. I wondered how crazy I could make her just playing with them and not touching anything else. I'd have to torture her later. I had other plans for this evening. She ran her hands over my chest, enjoying the feel of each muscle. My stomach twitched at her touch. It was light like a feather but made my skin feel so hot.

I kissed down her neck, down her chest, and up and down her belly before going back up again. Her belly was one of my favorite parts of her. It was so soft and full. It wasn't a flat belly. This was the belly of a real woman. I stopped at her breasts, giving them ample attention. My tongue was like electricity making a fiery current connection that ran from my body to hers and back again.

Abigail reached down to unzip my pants. Reaching in, she gasped as she ran her hand along the length of my cock. I was getting harder under her touch. She began to rhythmically stroke me, making me groan.

"Take them off, please," Abigail whispered.

I looked at her for a moment. "Are you sure, Abi?"

Abigail kissed me, biting my lower lip. "Yes."

I gave her a wink as a smirk spread across my lips. "I will if you will."

"Take them off for me?" Abigail purred.

Fuck, she knew just how to push my buttons in the best way possible. I stood up and slowly took my jeans off. Never taking my eyes off of Abigail.

She giggled. "Somehow I knew you would be going commando.

I moved the coffee table away a little more towards the center of the room. I wanted space to move with Abigail. I kneeled down, and stroked her body from her neck all the way down to her toes. I tickled her feet and she jumped and fell into uncontrollable laughter the more I tickled. I smiled. Another fun point I could use to torture her with at a later date. I kissed my way up to her waist. I gathered her shorts in my hands and slowly began to pull them down.

She lifted her hips for me, allowing me to pull them down below her ass. I finished pulling them down her thighs and calves and then they were off. I took a moment and stared at her body. I wanted to memorize every curve, every roll, every dimple. I loved them all. "You are truly beautiful," I murmured as I moved my hands freely along her body. I kissed and licked my way up her body. I found her soft plump lips and softly placed mine over hers, giving soft sweet little kisses before adding more pressure. I bit her lower lip and she granted me access. I loved the way her tongue tasted and felt. It was a shame to leave it but I had another destination in mind. My tongue skipped its way down her body. Using my knee, I spread her legs apart. It had been a while since I had been intimate with a woman, and I suspected Abigail was in the same boat as me. But I knew how to make her body tingle like no other. She had given me a verbal yes, so I knew she wanted me, and now that I could feel how wet she was, I knew her body wanted me as well.

I dipped a finger between her slick lips, I let them glide along the inside of her lips before moving to my true destination. Her precious clit was already hot and throbbing. Abigail bucked and moaned as I began to stroke it. She raised her hips, wanting me to go deeper. "Patience, my sweet Abi," I huskily whispered.

Abigail gripped the blankets as my fingers played. Breathing heavily, I just knew she loved, as well as hated the teasing. I removed my fingers, brought them to my mouth, and licked them. I gave Abigail a wink. "Mmm, delicious. Better than I dreamed." I repositioned myself, kissing her belly. I breathed it in as I kissed every inch of her belly before moving my head between her legs. I parted her lips, letting my tongue give her a slow, long lick.

"Liam" Abigail moaned. She reached for my head, taking a couple of my curls between her fingers and started twirling them as she writhed beneath me.

I looked up at her as I stroked her thighs as my tongue explored her. I relished in tasting her honey and eliciting the moans and sighs that I knew were bringing her closer to the edge. I stopped just short of her release of pleasure. I gave her a moment to catch her breath before slipping two fingers deep inside her, allowing my nimble fingers to find what they were looking for.

Abigail arched her back and opened her hips wider to me, closing her eyes as she did.

I raised my head a bit, keeping my fingers moving. "No love, don't close your eyes. Look at me. I want to see you. Really see you." I moved up to kiss her. Allowing her to taste herself on my lips and tongue as my fingers worked their magic. I broke the kiss. "Eyes on me love." I moved my mouth back over her clit, fluttering my tongue against it.

I opened my eyes and watched him. No one had ever asked me to do that. I was surprised how it turned me on. Watching him pleasure me and make my body tingle, heat up, squirm in blissful desire was new and I wanted more, so much more. My breath became raspy as I tried to remember to just breathe and enjoy. My entire body was humming. It was almost like I was floating. I started to close my eyes out of habit.

Liam must have seen my eyes close because he stopped moving his fingers, and pulled them out a bit. My eyes immediately snapped open. He had lifted his head and was looking at me with an intensity in his eyes. "Stay with me, love. Don't close your eyes."

It wasn't a command, but it wasn't a request either. I nodded as I bit my lower lip.

"Good girl." Liam winked and started moving his fingers as he lowered his head again.

I moaned loudly as his tongue tickled my clit. I was close to release. I could feel the familiar pull building up. I reached for Liam's free hand, never breaking eye contact with him. "Liam, I'm— oh god!" I clasped his hand, interlocking my fingers in his. I squeezed hard as my orgasm took over, cascading throughout my body. I looked into his eyes the whole time, allowing myself to freely express my pleasure in my very loud moans making the orgasm that much sweeter and longer. It had never been like this for me before.

As my orgasm began to subside Liam swiftly slipped his rock hard rod inside me, letting out a low, primal groan as he did. I loved the way my wet pussy walls enveloped his cock. And I think he liked it too. He filled me perfectly, like we were always meant to combine and become one. Liam started thrusting within me, rolling his hips to hit every angle. He clasped my hands, putting them over my head and pinning them there. Leaning down he took a nipple in his mouth, making it his own. All I could do was moan and submit, my hips started thrusting up to meet his.

Liam kept adjusting his speed from slow deep thrusts to fast and furious and back down again. He knew just how to prolong our first time. And bring me close to another orgasm. We were both sweating and letting off moans and groans that were primitive and guttural. In one last deep thrust he finally spilled his hot seed inside me. Pressing his thumb against my clit he gave one last thrust pushing his cum even deeper in me. That was all I needed to reach my own orgasm. I screamed his name with my own powerful release. Only briefly did I think about the fact we hadn't used a condom. And right then I really didn't care. I felt too damn good. He collapsed on top of me, still inside me. Both of us were out of breath. I smiled as I covered his face in sweet kisses.

"Will you stay the night?" I asked. I wanted to wake up with him.

Liam kissed my forehead then pulled out, before grabbing a blanket from the couch and wrapped the two of us in it. "As long as you don't care if I sleep in the nude."

I kissed him. "Not at all." I kissed him again, then started to snuggle down.

"Would you be more comfortable if we moved to your bedroom? Got into bed?"

I shook my head and smiled. "Not just yet. I'm good right here in our little love nest." I laughed "Sorry, that was really corny!"

"Corny or not, your wish is my command." He wrapped his arms around me as we snuggled down together. I don't know when we fell asleep.

The next morning, still in our nest, I was awoken out of a wonderful dream by a very loud knock on my front door. It startled me. Liam wrapped his arms around me tighter, in a protective move, yet he was still asleep. Sometime in the middle of the night Lochlan and Beartice had joined us. They were currently curled up behind Liam's back. The knock grew louder, I gently moved Liam's arms, got up and slipped my pajamas back on. I quietly walked to the front door. "Who is it?" I whispered.

"It's me! Open up, I brought breakfast," Tess barked through the door.

I groaned as I looked back at a sleeping Liam. He had begun to stir at the commotion. "Hang on just a minute!"

I went and kissed Liam to wake him up. He pulled me

down as he kept kissing me. I wanted to keep kissing him. I really liked kissing him. I wanted to start my day with him coming inside me again. But instead we had to deal with my best friend Tess. I begrudgingly pulled away from Liam. "My friend Tess is here. She has breakfast. I'm sure it's because she knows you are here, and wants to check you out."

Liam smiled. "This is best friend Tess, yes?" Liam asked as he stretched his body.

I nodded as I watched his long arms and legs reach even further in a deep stretch. I licked my lips at the thought of kissing him from head to toe. I thought about what his cock might feel like in my mouth. Maybe later. "Best friend in the world." I laced my fingers through his.

Liam gave me one more lingering kiss. "Well then, I better put some clothes on." Liam grabbed his clothes and headed to the bathroom. I went to open the door as I heard the shower turn on.

"Took you long enough," Tess started as she pushed her way into the kitchen and searched around looking for a glimpse of Liam.

"Good morning to you too. And he's in the shower so stop straining your neck."

"Oh, okay." Tess started emptying her bags. "So I'm not interrupting anything then."

I crossed my arms over my chest."What exactly are you doing here?"

"Well, I figured the only way I would get to meet your hunky man in person was if I just popped on over. I thought one of my world famous breakfasts would soften the blow." Tess laughed.

"You just couldn't wait a couple of more visits could you?" I chuckled, trying to hide my annoyance.

"Um no, he lives too far away for that."

"Lives too far away for what?" Liam asked as he walked into the kitchen. He was rubbing his hair with a towel to get out the excess water. He draped the towel over the chair and put his arms out to hug Tess. "Tess, I'm so glad you are here. I've heard so much about you."

Tess hugged him back. "Back at you. Let me just say I'm a big fan of your work. And I brought food to make one of my world famous breakfast meals, I hope you're hungry."

Liam gave her a great big smile. " World famous? I can't wait. I'm starving. Let me help you unpack."

Tess raised an eyebrow and looked at me. "He helps in the kitchen?"

I nodded. "He's good like that."

"What else is he good at?" Tess smirked as she looked Liam up and down.

I slapped her arm. "I will throw you out if you don't behave."

"Now, now Abi, that's no way to treat your best friend. Besides, how else am I going to learn all of your secrets?" Liam winked at Tess.

"Sorry Liam, my lips are sealed. Breakfast is all you will get out of me."

Liam gave her a wink. "We'll see about that."

I sat and watched as Liam and Tess unpacked all the groceries and started cooking. Tess was the chef and Liam her sous chef. I drank in the beauty that was my best friend and the man I was dating, getting along so well. It made my heart warm.

"Love, we are almost done here. Would you mind setting the table?"

I nodded as I got up and gave Liam a quick kiss before going into the dining room to set the table for three. Liam and Tess started bringing the food just as I finished.

Liam pulled out a chair for me. "Have a seat my lovely, let me make you a plate."

"Thank you." Another moment of blushing I was glad he couldn't see.

"Wait! You're making a plate for her?" Tess pretended to swoon. You wouldn't happen to have a single brother would you?"

Liam laughed as he shook his head. "No brother, just two sisters I'm afraid. One older and one younger. The older one is already happily married with a baby on the way. But my younger sister is single."

"That works too. How young?"

"Tess!"

She shrugged. "What? It doesn't hurt to ask."

"Can we just eat please?" I gave her my *knock that shit off* look.

She gave me a slight nod. "I bought orange juice and champagne. Who wants a mimosa?" Tess didn't wait for an answer. Instead, she went into the kitchen and made one for each of us.

"So Tess, tell me a juicy secret about Abi and I'll give you an EverMorph spoiler. Abi mentioned you watch the show."

Tess's eyes lit up as I could see her racking her mind for a juicy memory. I knew her too well.

"Don't you dare Tess!"

"But, but a spoiler!" Tess looked from me to Liam and then back to me again.

I laughed and shook my head. I knew she would never betray my trust.

Tess was true to her word and didn't spill any juicy secrets even though Liam tried a couple more times as we ate. He even dangled an introduction to his sister after he showed her a picture of her. Her name was Chloe and she was gorgeous and she was only a year younger than Liam. She would be perfect for Tess, age wise at least.

Two hours passed in the blink of an eye. Tess pushed her chair back from the table and began gathering up the dishes and bringing them to the kitchen. Once the table was clean she turned to us, hands on her hips. "Okay kids, I won't take up anymore of your time. I know this is a short visit." She went to give Liam a hug good-bye.

"You don't have to leave because of me, Tess. I'll be around for a long time if Abi can stand me." He winked at me.

Tess laughed. "Oh I know you'll be around a good long while. That's why I don't mind leaving now. I see a bright future for you kids." She gave me a hug. "Once he's gone I want all the juicy details," she whispered in my ear. She turned back to Liam. "Have fun, oh and feel free to give your sister my number. Ta-ta for now!" Tess headed out the door. A moment later she popped her head back in. "Oh, and if you two love birds go out today, may I suggest going out the back? There are some paparazzi waiting in the front."

I was shocked. "What? How?"

Tess tried to downplay it. "Don't worry it's only like two guys." She blew me a kiss as she closed the door behind her.

I started to wipe down the table. Liam wrapped his arms around me. "I like Tess." He kissed her neck.

I hugged his arms around me. "She likes you too. But not as much as I do."

"So, do you want to stay in, or embrace the big bad world?" Liam asked as he nuzzled my neck.

"Both." I whispered as I put his finger in my mouth, and started sucking on it.

Liam groaned. "Oh woman, you've done it now."

I sucked it a minute more than gave it a little bite before removing it from my mouth. "I turned to him and took my top off. " I need to shower." I kissed him and started to move towards my bathroom. I knew he was following me when I heard the zipper on his jeans go down.

~ LIAM ~

The weekend passed by far too quickly for my liking and I was already brainstorming for the next time I could see Abigail. She kissed me goodbye one last time before I headed to the airport.

"Are you sure I can't drive you?" She asked as she gave me big, sweet doe eyes. I had learned it was her way of getting me to do what she wanted. That, and sticking her lip out in the cutest pout I have ever seen in my life. I was complete puddy when she did that. Luckily it had only appeared twice over the weekend.

"No, the goodbye would be too hard. Besides, it's not like you can wait at the gate with me. This is better. And I promise to call you as soon as I land." I gave her one final kiss and left. I hadn't even used my hotel rooms that I booked . But I still had a few things there I needed to pick up. It was good to keep the paparazzi off my ass. They had found out I was staying there so I made sure to be seen coming in and out several times by myself. No need to pull Abigail into the ugly side of my world sooner than she needed to be. Once I officially checked out I called a car and headed to the airport.

Ted picked me up from the airport. He threw my bag in the trunk before getting in. "Thanks for picking me up, mate."

"Not a problem. We got back in earlier this morning. Connie gave me strict instructions to bring you home for dinner. She wants to hear all about this mystery woman who has you racking up frequent flier miles."

I chuckled. "It was one hell of a weekend man!"

"So you'll be going back?"

A big smile spread across my face. "Oh hell yes, I'll be going back."

"Sounds like you have a lot to tell us."

I looked out the window. "Aye."

"Well, I'm happy for you man. Can't wait to hear all about it."

When I walked into my class on Monday they were all huddled in a corner looking at something. I sighed, cell phones were going to be the death of me. "Alright hand over the cellphone. You know my rules about those."

"But look Ms. Reese. It's your dinner date. Did you know he had a kitten?"

"That was weeks ago! Why is it of interest now?" Mark questioned.

"Because this article is about his kitten. They just used a picture of him and Ms. Reese. It's called clickbait." Sharon was very matter of fact.

As I watched the scene play out in front of me I saw my lesson plan fade away like a watercolor painting that had been left out in the rain. I needed to bring this back around to the class topic. In the past weeks I had learned the best way to get back on task was to answer their questions As directly as I felt comfortable with and then move them along to the lesson plan at hand. "Yes, I did know that. He adopted the kitten which he named Aoife at the fundraiser event."

"Aoife? What kind of name is that?!" Jason questioned.

"Did you work your magic and persuade him to get the kitten?" Heather giggled.

Okay, that question needed somewhat of an indirect answer, "Aoife is an Irish name. If I'm not mistaken it means beautiful. And no, I did not work any magic. I merely suggested."

"Ha! Holy shit! Ms. R got a star to adopt a kitten. Wait till I tell my sister. She's gonna beg to be in your class in 2 years. You'll be her hero. Six degrees of separation, and all that." Keith laughed.

I clapped my hands loudly as I walked to the center of the room. "Alright, alright that's enough! Put the phone away and get out your Chaucer books."

Margo raised her hand.

"Yes Margo?"

"Have you been on another date with him?"

I pursed my lips holding in the large sigh I wanted to release into the classroom and the urge to beat my head against the chalkboard. "He works in Canada Margo. It's not like it's a short drive."

"Yes, but he has a place in New York and that *IS* just a short car ride away." Margo smiled

"Short?" Jason snorted.

"Well, shorter than a drive to Canada. And I read they had a mini break recently."

I chose to ignore Margo. Maybe if I went into full teacher mode they would stop with all the questions. "Clearly you are reading too many tabloids and not enough Chaucer. Sounds like a pop quiz is in order." There was an audible groan in the room and a couple of *Thanks Margo* comments.

"Everyone, get out a piece of paper and a writing utensil. Ten questions, each worth ten points. And yes, this will count towards your final grade in this unit." I gave myself an invisible high five. Order had been restored.

AND THAT'S ALL I HAVE TO SAY ABOUT THAT!

ALL THINGS EVERMORPH ALL THE TIME

SEASON FOUR

- **Episode Highlights:** A new story arc is brewing, centered around the disappearance of Flint, but the season is almost over? Will it spill into next season? Isla learns about the affair!! (well kinda sorta affair)
- **Episode Lowlights:** It's becoming more and more obvious that Queen Ryla is an inconsistent character in the EverMorph world.

My humblest apologies to you my loyal Everrites and Morphlings for this late chit chat. But I am here now so let us chit and chat shall we? Up first.........FLINT!!!! Where is our dearest Flint and who has him? All I could glimpse from the last episode is that someone or something is holding him captive. And whatever it is has a dark foreboding energy. Come on all my Flint Fairies, any guesses? Put them in the comments. I have a theory or two of my own, but I'm keeping them to myself for the time being. But I will tell you it's a doozy and very out of the box! However, the REAL question has become: is Lochlan going to journey on to help save the human race from the Morphlings? Or is he going to abandon his quest, and go save his best friend and head of the guard? Decisions, decisions!!

And I'm going to do it again. I'm going to pick on the writers. They need to make up their mind if the Queen is for saving the human race like her royal family wants and has decreed? Or does she want them decimated and enslaved like the Morphlings do. She seems to be flipping back and forth and back and forth!! OR, are the writers crafty beyond belief and they are setting us up for something HUGE! Ah!! The possibilities. Alright, enough of my blather. Share your thoughts!

Until next time EternallyEvers OUT!!

COMMENTS :

IFollowFlint: I'm torn. I feel it might be a faction of the morphlings who are holding him. But I thought I heard a woman's voice and it WASN'T Zarina!

LochlanIsMine: It has to be the Morphlings. They'll do anything to win the war. Taking Flint out of the equation gives them the upper hand.

Morphing4Oberon: I agree with you LIM it has to be the morphlings. I mean we know it's not the humans. They are too stupid to even know their existence is at risk. Who else could it be?

~ ABIGAIL ~

The next month flew by. Auditions had gone well. Margot and I were really happy with our cast choices. And rehearsals were going like clockwork. I was really proud how the cast had embraced the material and were each making it their own but working as a unit. I was sure it would be one of the best shows the school had done in a very long time. And Margot had taken to directing like a fish to water.

Spring break was close and I was as bad as my students silently counting down the days. Margot came up to me after English class. "Miss Reese, I have a question."

"What can I help you with?"

"Can we use your classroom after school today?"

"Who are we?"

"A couple of us from the show want to go over two scenes from the second act. But the auditorium is being used by the debate club. They have a match or meet or whatever it's called tonight. So they are rehearsing after school."

"How many of you?"

"It'll be me and four others."

"Sure, I can give you guys two hours."

Margot smiled, giving me a happy little hop. "Thanks so much! I hope we aren't keeping you from something else. I know as our advisor you need to be there. We really appreciate it."

"Not at all, Margot. It's my pleasure. If you guys are taking the initiative to rehearse on your own, far be it from me to dampen that kind of enthusiasm."

There was no way I was going to squash ambition or dedication. The final bell rang and the small group promptly showed up in my room. Ready to work.

"Do you want me to help direct or -"

"No thank you Ms. Reese. We've got this. But if you see something really bad please stop us."

I nodded. "Of course, but I don't think that will be a problem." I smiled as I took a seat behind my desk and took out some papers to grade, leaving them to their work.

When the impromptu rehearsal was over, I headed to *Marcone's* for my weekly dinner with Tess. Tess was already there and from the multiple glasses on the table I could tell she had already ordered drinks for us.

"Sorry I'm late. I had a last minute rehearsal to attend." I sat down and took a sip of my well placed amaretto sour.

"Sounds like the kids are really getting invested."

I nodded. "I was really worried because so many of them wanted to do a musical, but they are full steam ahead. I couldn't be happier."

"And how is Chaucer going?"

"So much better!" I practically squealed. " It took them a few tales to get into a good flow, but now they are really moving through it. I knew they would like it once they got started." I picked up my menu and started looking to see what I wanted to order.

"I think you need to take some of that credit. You are a really great teacher. You have a way with your students. They'll be sorry when you leave."

I put my menu down. "Leave? I have no intentions of leaving. What would make you think that?"

"I just assumed with who you are dating that you would be making a move sometime in the near future?" Tess gave me a sly smile.

I shook my head and laughed. "Wow! Talk about jumping to conclusions.

Tess took a drink, shaking her head. "I'm not conclud-ing, I'm deducing?"

I raised an eyebrow. "Alright, deduce me. This should be good."

Before Tess began her deducing, our server, Adam, came to take our order.

"Are you lovely ladies ready to order?"

"Well, aren't you a charmer?" Tess said in her sexy voice. "I'm feeling a little spicy tonight so I'll have the shrimp linguini fra diavolo. Make it extra spicy please."

"Extra spicy, I think I can handle that. He gave Tess a seductive smile. He then turned his attention to me. "And for you?"

"I'll have a sirloin steak medium rare with the sauteed broccoli and fully loaded baked potato as my sides."

Adam nodded. "We can make that happen. Can I refresh your drinks?"

Tess answered for the both of us. "Absolutely, thank you." She waited for him to walk away. Once he was gone,

Tess continued. "First, you and Liam had a strong connection from the word go. I actually wish I had been there to see it. I bet there were visible sparks, but I digress. Second, you guys talk every day! I mean who does that?! Even you and I don't talk every day."

I smiled. Tess hadn't said anything that wasn't true. "Is that all you have?"

"I have one more fact that is completely indisputable."

"And that is?"

"That I have never seen you happier in the twenty years that I have known you than you are right now. And that right there is enough to prove my point." Tess gave a triumphant laugh.

I couldn't dispute the truth. "You know, he invited me up to Canada to spend my spring break with him."

"Well! That is a new development that I can get behind. Dish please!"

"There is nothing to tell really. He asked me last night."

"And? Don't play games with me, woman! Are you going?"

"Of course I am!" I laughed. "It'll be my first trip to Canada, I'm very excited."

"I'm sure you'll have a wonderful time. And I expect pictures! Especially if you can get some from the set!"

I could feel my eyebrows furrow and my smile start to fade. I took a long sip of her amaretto sour. She waved the server over to get her another one. "I'm thinking about giving up my blog."

Tess almost spit out her lemon drop martini. A little dribbled out of the left side of her mouth. She quickly wiped it away. "I'm sorry, what?!"

I started to play with the corner of the tablecloth. "I

think I need to stop. I mean, Liam still doesn't know the truth. Now it feels a little wrong every time I write a new one. I feel like I'm betraying him or something."

"Betraying him? That's ridiculous. What makes you feel like that? He isn't talking bad about his fans, is he?"

"No, no! It's nothing like that."

Tess sighed. "You haven't told him, have you?"

I shook my head.

Tess took my hand. "Look, I understand that you want to tell him the truth and you seem to be struggling with it."

I nodded.

"So tell him about the blog, and then immediately tell him why you hid it from him. The whole truth. If he is really the guy that I think he is, all will be fine."

I looked at Tess. "And if it's not?"

Tess shrugged. "Then he's not really the guy for you, is he?"

"You make it all sound so simple." I snickered.

Tess cocked her head to the side. "Isn't it?"

All of a sudden I didn't feel comfortable having this conversation out in the middle of a restaurant. "Um, would you mind getting our food to go so we can finish talking at my place. I feel a little exposed at the moment."

Tess nodded as she waved for Adam. "Adam dear, there's been a change of plan."

Tess made herself comfortable as I made plates or our still warm food and brought them into the living room.

Tess was not a dining room girl most of the time. She was far too casual for it.

"Just rip off the bandaid and tell him you're a fan." Tess sipped her wine as she lounged on my couch. "What's the worst that could happen? I mean he already likes you right?" She scratched Lochlan behind his ears, getting a soft purr out of him.

"Right, but do you remember what happened BEFORE he dated Bianca Monroe? He met and ended up dating a fan when he was doing the show *Research Cove*. And that fan ended up selling information to the tabloids. They dated for a year, and she had been dropping tidbits to the tabloids from like the six month mark! She even spilled details about his sexual preferences."

Tess raised an eyebrow at me. "You mean his kinks? No one cares about preference so you have to be talking about kinks."

I pursed my lips. "I mean preferences."

Tess stifled a laugh. "Tomato, tomahto. Okay, continue."

"When he found out, he broke up with her and sued her. He won, and on the steps of the courthouse he publicly vowed to never date another fan again. It was a dramatic moment, all caught on film. It was a nightmare. He finished out the season but didn't return for the next. He dropped out of the television for a while after that. How could you not remember this?"

Tess cringed. I wasn't a fan of his until after I saw him on The EverMorphs. I never watched his movies or other series before that. Sorry." She shrugged and started eating her linguini.

I clenched my fists as I started pacing around my living

room. "I know I told you about this when it happened! Good to know you actually listen to your best friend when she talks to you." I spat.

"Hey! That's not fair! That was years ago! You're clearly hangry, so eat!"

I plopped down in my comfy armchair. "I know, I'm sorry. I just don't know what to do."

Tess handed me my glass of wine. "You just tell him. If you don't, it will come out anyway and he'll think you lied on purpose. Are you lying on purpose?"

"No!!" I chugged my wine, which is never a good thing to do. "I just, it kinda just snowballed on me and now. -" my throat burned.

"And now you are falling in love with him, and are scared it's too late?"

"Yes," I whispered "I am."

"Did you ever think that if you tell him the truth you'll also be freeing yourself? Shedding the past once and for all?"

Tess came over and gave me a hug. "You both deserve a happily ever after."

~ ABIGAIL ~

I tossed and turned all night. Even in my dreams I couldn't escape the memory. My mind brought me back to when I was seventeen and everything changed.

I was so excited. Over the last two years I had paid my dues working at the Sci-Con event that was held every year at the convention center in Rodendin. It was only thirty-five minutes from where I lived so my wonderful dad had no problem dropping me off and picking me up. He had been to enough Soap Opera conventions with me since I was ten that when I got into the science fiction genre, he couldn't take it anymore. He was proud of me and my maturity. He trusted me enough to go it alone at the conventions that were close by. I wasn't allowed to go to any night events, but I didn't mind.

This year I was a guide to one of the stars appearing. Even though I was only seventeen, I had shown such maturity over the past two years that my supervisors thought I was up for the task. It really helped that I looked and acted a couple of years older than

I was. I had always been an old soul, or so my grandmother had told me.

I had just touched up my make-up before heading to the waiting pen to be introduced to my charge for the day. I was rounding a corner when I heard two voices. I slowed down because I recognized the voices. One was Ryan Motlen and the other was Courtney Whelan, two of the stars of **The Lost Continent.** The show was in its second season and had already been renewed for two more seasons by the network. It had a huge following since season one and it didn't seem to be losing momentum. The actors had become an overnight phenomenon and were gaining more and more fans with each episode, and I was one of them. I took a step forward but was blocked from their view by a bit of a corner and some plants. I could see them, but from the way they were standing, they couldn't see me.

"Don't get me wrong I love being on this show and the money I'm making is on point!" Courtney mentioned.

Ryan nodded. "Right? My agent just got me a pay bump for the next two seasons and let me tell you it's a sweet one!"

"Shit! I need to get my agent on that! If I have to keep smiling and laughing at all these freak fests, plus all the work the show requires, I definitely want more money for the next two seasons too."

"I'm having a great time with the fans." Ryan laughed.

It was a throaty laugh that gave me a bit of a shiver.

"Ack! I'm all for having fans, I mean they are a great ego boost and all. But I did my time on a soap opera and those idiots could never separate me from my character. Or worse, the ones that could, actually thought they knew me! Like really? All they knew was whatever garbage I spewed out at an interview," Courtney scoffed.

"Ha! Interviews are my favorite. Give them a few hard knock

stories about your youth or early career and just watch the gifts
start rolling in."

"Hard Knocks? You grew up in an affluential family and had
everything you wanted including two very attentive parents, who
are wonderful by the way. Your dad makes the best barbecue and
your mom! Best cookies ever. You were one lucky kid!"

"You know that, and I know that. But the female fans who
send me gifts even though I make more money in a year than they
will in ten, don't know that."

Courtney playfully hit Ryan. "You're so bad."

"Don't you know it!" Ryan grabbed Courtney up into a kiss.
They stayed like that for a moment when Courtney broke away.

"Stop! You know the show would kill us if anyone found out
about us yet."

Ryan took a step back. "Ugh, I hate that we have to keep this a
secret."

Courtney touched his cheek. "Just until the end of the season.
It's not that much longer."

He kissed her palm and let it go. "Come on, we need to get back
to the pen room. Time to meet our handlers."

"Whoopee!" Courtney twirled her finger in the air. "I hope I
don't get stuck with some super fan."

Ryan laughed. "Don't you know my sweet, all the handlers are
super fans. They just couldn't afford to buy tickets to see us. So
now, they get to work for us for a day. So, try to be nice. And if you
can't then nice be fake, otherwise the show will fine you."

"I think I'll go for the latter." Courtney shrugged.

"Do your best. But you know it's the quiet ones that you
have to watch out for. They're the ones with the blogs and all
the fanfiction." Ryan pulled out his phone. "Speaking of blogs,
you've got to see this one, it's called Continent Confessions. It's
pretty racy at times, but has a good number of followers.

Although it's clearly run by a teenage girl. She calls herself JakesMyEvery."

Courtney looked at the phone. "Her every what?"

"Her every sweet dream I suppose." Ryan chuckled.

"Gross!" Courtney laughed. "Look, look! She ends each blog post with a tagline - until we drift together again, JakesMyEvery OUT!"

"See, she clearly has a crush on me. I'm sure a hug and kiss from me would give her quite a thrill."

Courtney lightly punched his arm. "The only woman you can give any kind of intentional thrill to is me, and don't you forget it."

"Yes dear." Ryan gave Courtney a coy little smile and batted his eyes.

They both laughed as they wandered into the holding pen area.

I couldn't believe what I had heard. Did everyone feel the same as they did? Probably not, but I was sure there were more like them. More than I'd like to admit. I took a few deep breaths and pulled myself together. I had a job to do, and even with this slap of reality, I had a responsibility I wasn't about to renege on.

Head high, back straight and shoulders squared, I walked into the holding room and found my supervisor.

"Ah Abi, just in time. Let me introduce you to who you will be helping today." Much to my disappointment Mark led me over to Ryan Motlen. "Ryan, I would like you to meet Abi. She is one of our best. She'll be assisting you today."

Ryan grabbed my hands in his. "Well it's wonderful to meet you. We are going to have a great day. I've been looking forward to this event all month. So tell me about yourself."

My mouth felt dry and my stomach a little sour. All I could do was smile and say "Hi."

Mark looked at me as if asking if I was okay. I gave him a slight nod and smile. "It's nice to meet you, Mr. Motlen. I have your schedule for the day. It includes your breaks so please let me know if there is anything I can get for you.

"Well you can start by calling me Ryan, please."

I gave him a curt nod. "Okay, Ryan then."

Ryan looked at Mark. "So serious this one." He gave me a smile.

"Oh she's a great employee. I'm sure once your day starts, you'll see." Mark nodded. "You should ask her about her blog. She writes one for your show. It's very entertaining."

"Oh really?" Ryan grinned. "I'd love to read it."

I could see Courtney out of the corner of my eye. She was stifling a laugh and rolling her eyes at Ryan.

Unfortunately Ryan and Courtney had joint sessions all day except for one. So I was forced to be close to Ryan as well as Courtney. Many times they whispered to each other or mouthed the words 'until we drift together again' and then snicker. I silently fumed when they would mention in their panels how they thought fan blogs were awesome and how they loved to read them, and sometimes even commented under secret names. I knew it was all a lie. I knew they were just making fun of the fans who had shown them nothing but love and devotion. Eventually I couldn't take it anymore.

Ryan and I, along with Courtney and her handler, Beth, walked down the hall from a session they had just finished to the break room for their twenty minute respite. A fan stopped them in the hall. Beth went to stop them but Courtney put her hand up signaling it was okay.

"Hi, I'm Nicole, I was just in your last panel. And you said you liked to read blogs." The nervous teen handed a piece of paper to Courtney. "Here is mine, maybe you guys can take a look sometime."

Courtney gave the girl a forced smile. "Of course! Ryan and I would love to! Right Ryan?"

Ryan moved next to Courtney giving Nicole a squeeze on the arm and a million dollar smile. "Absolutely, thanks so much. Maybe Cort and I can check it out on our break."

"Really?" Nicole was elated.

It broke my heart and made my blood boil at how excited that girl was, over such a huge lie.

"They are lying to you Nicole." I blurted out. "They won't look. And if they do, it will just be to make fun of you." My voice was low and tempered as I tried my best not to explode.

"Excuse me?" Courtney was visibly offended.

Nicole looked confused. She looked back and forth between Courtney and myself. "What? Really? But then why did they say—"

"Because they are horrible liars!" I exploded.

Ryan reached for me. "Abi, sweetie, I don't know why you are saying this but—"

I slapped his hand away. "Because I heard you, both of you laughing and mocking your fans."

Ryan and Courtney looked at each other. Courtney swallowed hard while Ryan tried very hard not to look guilty. A crowd had begun to gather.

The flood gates had opened. I couldn't hold back anymore. "I believed in you, we believed in you. Became engrossed in your character's world and in turn became fans of the actors who portrayed them. You know some people here have saved all year just to have the chance to be in the same room as you, get an autograph and maybe a picture if they've saved up enough. And all you can do is laugh at us, look down on us, and make hateful mean comments about us. You are the worst of the worst!" At this point my voice was a full octave above a screech.

"Listen here Abigail, you need to stop lying," Courtney huffed.

"You're the liar, not me!" I shouted. I started to pace. I couldn't believe this self absorbed bitch called me a liar! "Let's see Courtney, you think your fans are an ego boost for you, but otherwise you can't stand them. And you!" I turned to Ryan, "You try to get gifts from them even though how did you put it, you make ten times what they do?"

Ryan gave off a chuckle like he was trying to diffuse the situation. He smiled at me, not reaching for me, but leaning in a bit closer. "Let's take this conversation into the break room, shall we? I'm sure it's just been a miscommunication."

Miscommunication my ass! I thought to myself. It took everything within me not to push him away. "Until we drift together again. It's what the two of you have been joking and snickering about all damn day! That's my blog asshole!"

"Continent Confession! I love that blog!" Nicole chimed in.

"You've been making fun of me ALL day! ALL day! And I've taken it because that's my job. But now you are lying to Nicole and I say enough! You are both disgusting, terrible human beings and I hope your characters both get killed off! You've ruined the show I love with your evilness and feelings of superiority. You seem to think you are better than any of us, but you aren't! You disgust me!" I spat at their feet and started to walk away. No one needed to tell me I was fired. A few fans that had gathered clapped in agreement before walking away themselves. I walked out of the convention center and called my dad to pick me up. No one noticed that Beth had filmed the entire incident. No one noticed until it was online later that night.

I gasped as I sat straight up in bed. I wiped the sweat off of my face with the bottom of my night shirt. I got up to splash some water on my face, and took a long drink of cold water. I sighed. My mind forced me to relive it over and over. Fifteen years had passed and yet here I was. How was I ever going to be able to tell Liam? *The Lost Continent* had run for another four years. I had never watched another episode and had shut down my blog when I got home that day. I also had never stepped foot in another fan event of any kind.

- BLOG SPOT -

AND THAT'S ALL I HAVE TO SAY ABOUT THAT!

ALL THINGS EVERMORPH ALL THE TIME

UPDATE REMINDER

Hello my dear sweet Everriles and Morphlings. Surprise!! An unexpected, and super short blog just for you. Oh Yae! Oh Yae! Here is your official reminder of the grand contest that the Queen and her favorite son are putting forth to us, their loyal subjects. All entries must be postmarked no later than next Saturday, not this one coming up, but the next. So get those applications (is it an application they are asking for? I never checked - oops!) out there! Remember to go to The EverMorphs official website for all the rules and the proper way to enter. I wish the best of luck to you all and hope the Goddess of Nyla blesses one of you wonderful readers with the winning invitation!

Until the next toe curling, mouth dropping episode - be well! Until next time EternallyEvers OUT!!

COMMENTS:

> BeatriceBabes: Thanks for the reminder! Updating a friend as I type!

~ ABIGAIL ~

I sat at my desk waiting for my students to finish their last test before spring break. I had given them the option: a major test before spring break with no homework. Or no test, and a project due upon their return from spring break. They had voted and had unanimously chosen the former. One by one as they finished their test they came up and left it on my desk and took a donut. I always plied them with sugar after a test. They need a sweet to go with the bitter.

"Five minutes left, people."

Andrew raised his hand.

"Yes Andrew?"

"So absolutely no homework over the break, right?"

I smiled. "Yes Andrew, no homework over the break. However—"

There was an audible groan across the room as the last students brought up their test. I got up and moved the panel on the chalkboard to reveal the details of their

Canterbury project. "This is the project that you will be assigned the first day you get back. It will be due two weeks later. Now, if you want, you can start it on your vacation. There will be no extra points, early grading or special consideration given to those of you who decide to start this on their vacation. I just wanted you to have the option."

"So we really don't have to start this until we get back?" Tori asked with suspicion in her voice.

I nodded as I held back a laugh. " That's right, you don't. You don't even need to write this down if you don't want to, I'll be giving this same information to you when you get back. But in the meantime, I have more donuts so please help yourself. Now, with the last of the tests in, what I really want to hear are any good plans you may have for the break."

"What about you, Ms. Reese? Any big plans?" Margot asked with a sly smile on her face.

She, like many of my other students, speculated that I was dating Liam Caffney. They would show me a blurry tabloid photo, or ask a question every once in a while, but I never answered them, only smiled and changed the subject. So they never had solid proof. Not that they hadn't been digging for dirt. But Liam and I were very careful. Yes, there had been a few shots here and there, but never in a compromising position. We often looked like two friends palling around.

"I asked about *your* plans Margot, not mine." I smiled.

"My family is going to Florida to visit my grandparents. On my dad's side, not the nasty ones from my mom's side. And we are also going to Disney World and SeaWorld."

"Now that sounds like some nice plans. And since you answered my question. I'll answer yours. I am indeed going away on vacation."

~ LIAM ~

I sat in my trailer in what our cast lovingly referred to as the corral. It was funny because all of our trailers were in an oddly large semi circle instead of in rows. I guess they thought this could be something new and fun. I never knew what ran through the minds of the production team and executives, but it worked well for all of us.

I knew the lines for my next scene, but wanted to go over it one more time in my mind before I started shooting. I put some classical music on and closed my eyes. My lines moved like musical notes through my head as I listened. It was my secret weapon that helped me keep all the lines in my head. A knock on the door interrupted my flow.

I opened my eyes and took a sip of my tea. "Come in."

The door opened and Ted came in. Ted Rendfelt was my castmate and best friend. We have known each other for years, longer than the show had been running. "Hey, I have an official invitation for you."

"Oh really?"

"Well, it's not just for you."

I chuckled. "Okay, now you've piqued my interest."

Ted handed me a very fancy envelope. I raised an eyebrow at him. "A little fancy for a poker invite, don't you think mate?"

"Ha-ha! It's Connie. She's way into crafting at the moment. Just open it."

I opened the envelope to find an invite to a dinner party. "Oh, isn't this lovely!"

"She's really hoping you and Abi can make it. Secretly I think she's dying to check her out. Make sure she passes her test of worthiness for you."

I leaned back on my couch. "Trust me, she will pass. We'd love to come."

"Great! My uncle will be there too. He's in town for a show. They are actually bringing his show back, but with an all new cast. They got most of the original cast back to guide the new younger generation into the series."

"Really?"

"He thinks it's a ridiculous concept and will get canceled quickly. But if it doesn't, then it means some recurring work for him several times a season."

"I guess retirement didn't suit him?"

Ted snorted. "Not even close! He's been teaching the entire time, but he can't stay away from a camera."

"But wasn't that show on like fifteen, twenty years ago or something?"

"You know the saying - Everything old is new again."

"Is that really a saying?" I laughed.

Ted shrugged and started laughing.

"What was the name of the show he was on again?" I asked as he took a sip of his tea.

"It was called *The Lost Continent*."

There was a knock on the door. It opened and Piper, my favorite PA, poked her head in. "Liam, they are ready for you on set." She looked over and saw Ted. "You too, Mr. Rendfelt." She closed the door behind her.

"Mr. Rendfelt?" I questioned.

Ted shrugged. "I don't think she likes me very much. But she keeps it professional."

"You know, if you asked her to call you Ted, she would. That's what I did."

"Oh really? You asked her to call you Ted?"

"Oh man! Was that a dad joke? It sounded like a dad joke. Is there something you and Connie need to tell me?" I laughed.

Ted laughed and rolled his eyes. "If there is, it's a surprise to you and me both! First marriage, and then a baby, maybe." Ted opened the door to the trailer. "Come on, last shot of the day."

"Ah! So you've been thinking about popping the question to Connie." I clapped my hands. "That's great man!" I followed him out.

Ted gave me a wink and shrugged his shoulders. "I plead the fifth."

I nodded. "Alright mate, change of topic, only one more day until Abi is here."

AND THAT'S ALL I HAVE TO SAY ABOUT THAT!

ALL THINGS EVERMORPH ALL THE TIME

GONE FISHIN'

Alright you Everrites and Morphlings, this week's musings will be delayed a week. Sorry folks but even this Everrite needs to leave the land of the fairies every once in a while for a wonderful vacation with the mermaids! But never fear, I'll be back next week to discuss everything EverMorph from both episodes so get ready! Oh, and has anyone heard anything about who won the contest?

Until next time EternallyEvers OUT!!

COMMENTS:

NylaKingidon4Ever: Have a great vacation!

Morphing4Oberon: Mermaids?! Where did you go?!

IdolofIsla: Mermaids rule! Aren't they actually a type of fairy? How come there are none in Nyla? Can't wait to hear where you went.

IFollowFlint: Yup! They are! Maybe next season we'll see some!

~ LIAM ~

I met Abigail at the airport. I was waiting for her in the baggage claim area with a newsboy cap and sunglasses. I had my hair pulled back and a sign that read Miss Abigail Reese in a wonderful calligraphy. Connie had been nice enough to make the sign for me on short notice. I greeted her with an English accent. "Are you Miss Reese? Miss Abigail Reese? My name is Giles and I'll be your driver for the duration of your stay. Welcome to Toronto."

Abigail giggled but played along. "Well, it's nice to meet you, Giles. I just need to grab my luggage and we can go, yes?"

"Allow me to grab your bag, madam. What does it look like?"

"Why thank you, Giles. It's a black suitcase with two big yellow daisies on it. The front of the suitcase is cloth and the flowers are embroidered on it."

"Oh, you mean like that one?" I pointed at a suitcase coming across on the conveyor belt.

"Yes! That's the one." Abigail smiled.

I went and grabbed the bag. I came back with her bag in hand and offered my arm to Abigail. "Shall we ma'am?"

Abigail nodded. "That would be lovely."

I dropped the act as soon as we got to my car. "How was your flight, love?" I leaned over and gave her a soft kiss on the lips.

"It was great. I slept most of the way."

"And what about Casseopia and Dipper? Were they mad you left them?"

"Oh, I gave them lots of lovies before I left, and they always have a good time with their Auntie Tess. She spoils them more than I do. How was work?"

"It was great. Another day of fighting evil fairies and saving the human race. You know, the usual."

"You know, I actually started watching the show. I wanted to see what you were doing."

I gave her a side glance. "Really now? You started right from what is it? Season four that's playing now?"

Abigail shook her head. "I started from season one. I found it streaming on one of the internet platforms. I think it was FlixArt."

"Ah yes, the internet is a wonderful thing. And because it's so wonderful, we don't get residuals from that."

"Do you want me to stop watching?"

"Would you if I asked you to?" I was curious to know.

"Of course. But I don't know why you would want me to." I looked out the window. I really needed to stop lying. I thought mentioning the show would help me ease into the truth I wanted to tell him this trip. I wanted to do it first thing. I was firm on that. I needed to come clean and just let the chips fall where they may. But the moment had passed. Soon though, very soon.

"I would never ask that of you." Liam winked. "Just wanted to see how much under my spell you truly are."

"Oh, I'm under a spell, am I?" I moved my hand up and down his thigh and gave it a squeeze, before letting it rest there.

Liam chuckled as he swallowed hard. "Careful now."

"Oh, I'm sorry, I'll move it." I moved my hand even closer to his crotch.

Liam let out a low groan. "Abi, I'm driving."

I gave his thigh a squeeze again. "Then keep your eyes

on the road. And be careful." I grazed my hand over the growing bulge in his pants.

Liam let out an audible gulp and tried to steady his breath. "I thought I'd cook for you tonight since you were so nice and cooked for me last time."

"Oh! What are you making?"

"I have some steak filets marinating as well as some twice baked sweet potatoes with an herb butter ready to pop in the oven, and then I'll grill some asparagus with the steaks."

"That sounds delicious." I gave Liam's thigh another squeeze. "How long can the steaks marinate?"

Liam licked his lips and took a quick glance at me. "Long enough."

Liam was kissing me before he had the door locked. He had me pinned against the door as his tongue explored my mouth. I could feel his bulge growing against me the deeper he made his kisses. I moaned at the feeling and gyrated my hips against him "I've missed you, and I can feel you missed me." I reached down to stroke the bulge through his pants before unzipping them and reaching my hand down to fully grasp the rod that was awaiting my touch. He groaned, thrusting his hips towards my hand. He kissed me a moment longer and then pulled away with a final kiss. He took my hand and led me to the bedroom.

"Stay right there, love." Liam went back towards the front door. I stayed on his comfortable bed as I looked around the room. It was a large, but simple room. A king size bed with a nice down quilt in a lovely shade of green. There were four pillows on the bed. None were decorative. He had a long dresser opposite the bed and a large tv mounted above it. There was a wall of large windows that looked out onto the water. The opposite wall had some artwork framed and arranged nicely. Each piece was from a different artist, that much I could tell.

I heard the lock snap closed before he came back to the bedroom to find me exactly where he had left me. I was sitting on the end of the bed, still looking around his room. Liam stood in the door frame for a few minutes. I could feel him watching me as I looked around his room. I smiled and reached out my hands to him. "Come sit with me."

Liam took my hands, sat down next to me and kissed me. He started lifting up the top of my shirt, but stopped mid belly. "May I?"

I nodded and lifted my arms up. Liam lifted my shirt off and kissed me. He stood me up and kissed down my belly, stopping at my jeans. He unbuttoned them, then slowly pulled down the zipper as he looked into my eyes. I took his hair out of the ponytail it was in and ran my fingers through it. Liam pulled my jeans to the floor. Stepping out of them, he turned me around, giving me soft kisses down my neck and back as he undid my bra. I cooed at the feeling as it made me tingle like a slow rolling wave through my body, taking up every space with delicious desire.

Liam turned me to face him, and just looked at me. I loved the way he looked at me, I could see in his eyes how much he wanted me. And it made me want him more than I already did. He ran his fingers from the top of my head down to my toes. He made swirls with his fingers and also tapped when he wanted to. I loved the way the heat of his hands felt against my skin.

"You're so soft." he whispered. "Supple and full, so womanly. I can't stop touching you."

"Then don't." I murmured.

A few goose bumps rose under his touch. "Are you cold?"

I shook my head and huskily said, "No. Your touch just makes me quiver. I love the way your hands feel on me."

He smiled and kept touching me until he had worked his way back up to my head. He gently took my face in his hands and began kissing me again. First just the bottom lip then the top, then both. I bit his lower lip, drawing it into my mouth and giving it a little suck, making him groan. He wrapped his arms under my arms and pulled me close to him, deepening the kisses as he did. It caught me off guard and I sucked in my breath as I began to melt in his arms. He laid me on the bed and pulled my panties off.

~ LIAM ~

I loved watching Abi raise her hips to me as I pulled her panties off. I could see she was glistening, and could smell her arousal. It was like a sweet ambrosia to me. She was just waiting for the touch of my tongue, my fingers, or my throbbing cock. I licked my lips thinking which one would enter her first.

Moving her legs and nestling myself between them, I began to let my tongue play with her breasts. She moaned as she felt my warm tongue against her hardening nipple. I knew that was a sign she wanted my lips wrapped around them. I slowly moved into her as she arched her back, and let out a cry.

Abigail gasped as I went deeper. Letting my hard cock fill her up. Her folds held me deep within her. I smiled as I felt her walls around me, hot, wet, wanting me, taking me all in. We moved together like a current following the phases of the moon, waves of pleasure surging through us both, in sync with our moans and pleasurable touches. Legs entangling and arms roaming and eventually entan-

gling. In the end hands clasped together, forgetting everything around us except each other.

"Shit! I started to slow my pace. "I'm so sorry, in my
haste I forgot a condom! I need to pull out before I come,
and I'm so close." I couldn't believe I had allowed myself
to get so carried away. It wasn't like me. And I was mad at
myself. We had discussed this last time this happened, and
it was to be a one off. I should have been more considerate
of Abigail. I started to pull out, but Abigail wrapped her
legs around my waist and dug her nails into my back.

"No! I want to feel you come inside me. I want all of
you, no barriers." She kissed me. "Just you and me
together."

"Are you sure?" I looked into her eyes.

Abigail nodded. "Please." she whispered.

I could never resist her when she said please. "Eyes on
me love." I sped up, thrusting hard and shallow then slow
and deep. Her nails dug deeper into my back spurring me
on, until I let go, giving her all of me. I reached down and
rolled my thumb on her clit as I sucked her a nipple
bringing her over the edge clenching around my cock still
deep inside of her. I loved it when she screamed my name
and left red marks on my back.

We were satiated and content lying in each other's
arms.

Abigail played with one of my curls. Just twirling and
curling it between her fingers. Unable to erase the smile
from her lips.

"You seem happy." I smiled as I gazed at Abi's face.

She nodded. "You make me exceedingly happy."

"Are you hungry?" I began playing with one of her
braids. "I still have those steaks marinating."

Before Abigail could answer, her stomach answered for her with a loud rumbling making us both laugh. I gave her several kisses before getting up. I leaned over to grab my jeans.

"I can feel you staring at my ass." I laughed.

"It's a pretty fabulous one," Abigail stated.

I turned to her as I zipped up my jeans. "Do you want to help or stay here?"

Aoife meowed and jumped up on the bed. She walked over to Abigail and promptly began kneading her thigh before circling to make a comfortable spot. Abigail scooped the cat up in her arms giving it snuggles. "I think I'll stay here with Aoife for a bit. I'll join you as soon as she tells me how she likes living with you."

I gave the cat a scratch and a kiss on the head. "Now Aoife, don't go telling Mommy all of Daddy's secrets, okay?"

Abigail looked at me, but said nothing, she just smiled and blew me a kiss. "Us girls have to have our secrets. So why don't you go start those steaks Daddy, and we'll be right in."

I raised my eyebrow, but said nothing. I liked that she referred to me as Daddy when talking to my cat. Even if I had started it. After I said it, I was worried Abigail would freak out. But apparently I had nothing to worry about. She had just gone with the flow. I had never met someone like her. I would have to thank Arlene for making me go to that fan event. I gave Abigail a kiss and grabbed a tee shirt before heading out to the kitchen and then the balcony where my grill was.

~ ABIGAIL ~

I laid in bed a little while longer loving on little Aoife. She had grown a lot since I had seen her last, but it was obvious she was the runt of the litter. She'd always be small. Eventually I got up and put my clothes back on. I put my hair in a ponytail and scooped Aoife up. "So tell me Aiofe, does your daddy talk about me when I'm not here?"

Aoife meowed in response. "Oh he does, does he? All good things I hope?" Aoife began to purr in my arms. "I love him, you know," I whispered in the cat's ear. "And I think he loves me too." I let out a small giggle.

I walked into the living room and made myself comfortable. Liam had glass windows leading out to his patio. I watched him start up the grill and put the steaks on. He seemed to be enjoying himself. He was whistling as he worked. I got up and peeked my head out of the sliding glass door, kitten on my shoulder. "Want me to preheat the oven?"

Liam turned and smiled. "I see my two girls are getting along."

I gave Aiofe a pet. "Always."

"If you could set it to four hundred that would be perfect, love."

I turned to head to the kitchen. "I feel you staring at my ass." I laughed.

"It's a pretty fabulous ass." Liam chuckled. "I'd love to see it with a butt plug in it."

I slowly turned around and put the cat down. Liam had an amused look on his face but I could tell that he was serious. "You would?" I bit my lower lip, chewing on it out of nervousness.

Liam put his tongs down and moved toward me, wrapping his arms around me. "There are lots of things I'd like to try with you." He kissed my neck and caressed my ass. "I hope you'll share with me all the things you want to try. And we can decide together how and when we play together."

"You want to know my fantasies?"

Liam nodded. "When you're ready to share them."

"And you'll tell me yours?"

Liam raised an eyebrow. "Of course. I've already started. There's something about you Abigail Reese that makes me trust you completely. That's a rare feeling indeed. I plan to not question it and just enjoy it. Enjoy the trust we have."

The sincerity of his words left me breathless. I felt terrible knowing I was keeping something from him, yet he was being so vulnerable with me. I had to come clean and I had to do it before I left Canada.

- LIAM -

My alarm went off earlier than either of us would have liked. I had pulled several strings and was able to get Abigail on set with me for the morning. She had to leave after the lunch break, but it was a compromise I was willing to accept.

Abigail groaned as she rolled over, putting the comforter over her head. I knew she was an early bird, but even this was early for her. I pulled the cover off her head and gave her a kiss. "Up, up, we've got a busy morning."

"But it's my first day of vacation," Abigail whined.

"Well, if you don't want to go to the set with me today that's fine. I'll just see you when I get home tonight. Hopefully it won't be too late." I went to get out of bed.

Abigail grabbed my arm stopping me. "Wait, I get to go to the set with you? I can actually watch you film!?" She didn't try to hide her excitement.

I was pleased that she was excited. Even with her just starting to watch the show, I wasn't sure how interested she would be in watching me work. But since she taught drama I thought she might have an interest. Nothing big was happening today, no spoiling points, secret reveals, or cliff hangers. It's why the producers and director were pretty amenable to her being on set for the morning. "You'll have to sign an NDA and you'll need to leave after lunch. But yes, if you want to come watch you can."

Abigail jumped up and gave me a hug along with a big kiss. She looked at me with a mischievous look in her eye. "Do I have time to thank you properly for such a wonderful surprise?" She reached down and started stroking my cock through my boxer shorts.

I groaned and leaned into the tingles she was sending through my body. I bit my lip, debating on whether we had time. The things I wanted to do to her would require more time than we had. I knew that. But my mind went blank as I felt her hot breath on my growing staff, and then the wetness of her tongue as it wrapped itself around my tip gently sucking before engulfing all of me. My knees buckled and she grabbed my ass to help support me. She stayed like that, treating my hard cock like a big, long lollipop. Sucking all the great flavor out of it. As I was about to crest, I grabbed my head and thrust my hips, making her take me in even farther.

Abigail reacted by sucking and licking even harder making me explode and she drank all of me in, which was so fucking hot. She smiled as she wiped the corners of her mouth and got out of the bed. "Want some eggs for breakfast? Maybe a little bacon and some nice sliced fruit?"

I was silent as I tried to catch my breath. I grabbed for Abigail, pulling her into a kiss. "You can't do that and just walk away. I want more." I kissed her again, cupping her ass and kneading it.

Abigail sucked my tongue for a minute before pulling away. "I'm so excited for today."

"I'm excited too, Abi." I kissed her again.

Abigail pulled away. "Not that kind of excited." She giggled as I nuzzled her neck.

"Are you sure about that?" I reached my hand under her night shorts and cupped her core. Her panties were already wet. I nipped at her neck, knowing it would make it hard to resist me.

Her breathing became measured. "It can't be my fault that we are late today. I just wanted to give you a little thank you."

I sighed, Abigail had a point and I knew it. "Alright Abi, but when we get home you are all mine." I gave her a deep kiss before heading to the kitchen. "I'll make breakfast, why don't you jump in the shower?"

We made it to set on time. We were actually a little early so Abigail could sign her non-disclosure agreement. Once everything was signed, I was able to give her a quick tour around the set before heading to the costume and makeup trailers. Abigail followed me around, keeping very quiet. She smiled and nodded when she was introduced. She sat where Piper told her it was safe to sit.

I sat where Piper told me. I had a full view of the set but wouldn't be getting in anyone's way from this vantage point. I tried to be super cool and not let the inner child in me become overly giddy. I was quiet as a church mouse as they filmed. I had to remind myself to breathe because I kept holding my breath still in awe of where I was.

After the last scene broke, Liam and one of his coworkers walked over to me. Both had longer hair and fairy ears on. Liam also had wings that were closed and close to his back. My eyes became wide. It had been rumored that some of the Fae would have wings in either this season or the next season. So far there had been no sightings this season, but now I had solid proof. And I couldn't tell a soul. My inner fan was screaming. I told her to shut the hell up, and smile.

"Abi, this is my best mate Ted, he plays Flint on the show. And Ted this is Abi, the lovely woman I have been telling you about."

Ted walked up and gave me a hug. "It's so nice to finally meet you. I've heard so many wonderful things about you. I hope you know this lad is quite smitten with you."

"You can stop now, Ted!" Liam turned a little red in the cheeks.

"It's wonderful to meet you too, Ted. Liam speaks very highly of you."

"Lies, all of them I'm sure." Ted smiled. "Are you having a good time on set so far?"

I couldn't hide my awe and excitement. "This has been amazing so far. I am loving every minute of it."

Ted gave Liam a look. Liam just shook his head. "Well, I hope we'll see you later this week. My Connie is dying to meet you."

"Connie?" I looked at Liam.

"Yes, Connie is Ted's girlfriend. She invited us to dinner later this week."

"Oh! That would be nice." I smiled.

"You didn't show her the invitation, did you, you big loser."

Liam shrugged. "I meant to, but she just got in last night and it slipped my mind."

Ted laughed and nodded his head. "Okay, I get it, I understand. It's the only acceptable reason. Just make sure you show up."

Liam crossed his chest with three fingers. "Scouts honor mate, we'll be there with bells on."

Piper came over interrupting their conversation. "Liam and Ted, you are requested on set for places please."

Ted nodded. "Abi, nice to meet you. Enjoy your day. We'll talk later. I can give you all the dirt on this one."

"No, no he can't." Liam gently punched his arm. He

turned back to me. "Enjoy the show." He gave me a quick kiss and went on set.

I was in all my glory. I couldn't believe where I was sitting and what I was watching, it was like the ultimate dream. I watched and listened and absorbed everything I could. What amazed me the most was Liam. Of course I knew he was a great actor, his performances were proof of that. But I had never seen him in person, and it was beyond magic. He had such a gift, and talent. The cameras really didn't do his performances justice. I couldn't take my eyes off him.

Every time they stopped to reset something or because a line had been fumbled, I looked around at everything trying to memorize it all. The marks, the props, the pieces of green screen that would be filled in during post-production, the other actors and how they all interacted together not only when they were acting but when the camera wasn't rolling.

I was filled with love. Love for the show I had been a fan of for the last four years, love for Liam, and love for the process of it all. It fulfilled something in me I didn't know needed filling.

For me the morning passed quickly. They filmed until one in the afternoon, and then broke for lunch for an hour. Liam took me back to his trailer for lunch. When we walked in, there was a table with candlelight set up with two very large grilled chicken salads and sparkling lemon water in wine glasses. There was also a vase with six roses in it. Two yellow, two red, one pink, and one white.

"Oh Liam, this is lovely! How on earth did you have time to do this?" he never ceased to amaze me.

"Piper, the PA, is very good to me. I asked for her help,

and she was more than happy to assist when I told her it was for you." He pulled out a chair for me.

We ate lunch and then made out on the couch for a bit like two high school teenagers. Finally Liam pulled back." I'm afraid it is that time of day."

"NO! I'm having so much fun." I stuck out my lower lip and gave him a playful pout.

Liam laughed. "Oh no! That's not gonna work this time. But, I will see if I can wrangle another visit for you before you leave."

"I would love that." I gave him a big smile and a kiss. "I wish I had time to show how much I would love that." I kissed him again, cupping his ass.

"Show me when I get home. It won't be a late night."

"Famous last words." I laughed.

"No, it's a promise." Liam gave me an enticing kiss and a playful slap on my ass. He grabbed my hand. "Come on, let me walk you to security. I arranged for a car to pick you up." He reached in his pocket and pulled out a key on a maroon Evermorph key chain. "And this is for you. You're very own key to my apartment. Because you already have the key to my heart."

I had to bite my tongue not to say I love you. I didn't want to spook him, in case he thought it was too early to say.

He grabbed my flowers up in one hand and held my hand with the other. He waited with me until the car arrived.

"You have your keys, right?"

I nodded as I held them up. "Please tell your producer thank you. I had a really amazing time."

Liam nodded and handed me my flowers. "I will, I'll

see you at home tonight. I should be home by seven at the latest. If it's going to be later, I'll call you."

"Yes, and I will have dinner waiting for you. And something amazing for dessert."

Liam wrapped his arms around her. "Something more amazing than you?" He rubbed his nose against mine and then kissed me.

"You certainly know how to make me melt, Mr. Caffney."

Liam smiled. "I try my best." He kissed me one more time and squeezed my hand before closing the car door and heading back to set.

I was on cloud nine going back to the apartment. I was greeted by Aoife who was very happy to have someone home during the day. She immediately curled up as best she could in the crook of my neck and began to purr. I grabbed something to drink and my notebook. I went out on the balcony and started to write. My journal would help me capture every moment that had just happened.

The next morning I woke up in Liam's arms. My body was used to getting up early. The sun was just beginning to stream through his curtains. He had a soft little snore that actually reminded me of Aoife's purr. I stifled a laugh as I gently kissed his lips and slipped out of bed. I went to the kitchen to put some coffee on. I stooped over, looking in the fridge for some eggs and cheese to whip up an omelet when I felt something hard against my ass as two arms wrapped around me.

"Good morning, love."

"I see you are up and awake." I stood up.

"Aye, that I am." Liam kissed my neck and began sucking on it. That one act made me go weak in the knees.

"Don't, don't make me drop the eggs," I gasped. My voice became raspy the longer his lips lavished my neck.

"I have a big day planned for you." Liam spun me around and kissed me as he took the eggs and cheese from me and placed them on the counter to my right. He took my hand and led me back to the bedroom and leaned me back onto the bed. "And this is only the beginning." He kissed me several times before coaxing my mouth open with his tongue. I was up for whatever he had planned. But I did have a few tricks up my sleeve. As Liam was kissing me, I surprised him by flipping him over so that I was on top and he was under me. I pinned his hands above his head, much like he had done to me at my place. "My turn to show you a few things," I purred as I lowered myself onto his stiff shaft.

He groaned as he watched me slide lower, taking him in. "God, you feel amazing," Liam whispered as I gyrated my hips.

I leaned down and kissed him, letting my tongue dance with his. We spent the morning making love as the sunlight streamed in through the window.

By early afternoon we were in Liam's car. "Where are we off to?" I asked as I held his free hand as he drove.

"I thought we would go to the CN Tower. There is a beautiful view from the top and there is a restaurant where we can grab lunch before our next stop." He kissed my hand and smiled as he drove.

Baseball cap and sunglasses on, we headed to the top of the tower.

"The city is so beautiful!" I was wonderstruck. The view was as grand as the one from The Top of the Rock in New York City. I had to admit it was actually better since this view included the water. I closed my eyes, letting the sun hit my face.

"Perfect day for the view, isn't it?" Liam asked as he grabbed my hand.

I nodded, "Let's take a picture."

Liam used his long arms to take several really good

selfies of the two of us. We walked around a bit and I did
notice that people would nod at Liam or mention that
they loved him on the show in passing. But no one
stopped to ask for autographs or pictures. They kept a
respectful distance while expressing their admiration. I
wondered if it was a Canadian thing or if it was because so
many shows filmed there, the folks were used to seeing
actors from their favorite shows all the time.

After I had gotten my fill of taking pictures and
enjoying the views, Liam took me up one level to the
restaurant. We enjoyed a lovely lunch where again several
people gave Liam a nod or a wave. He was always gracious
and would nod, wave, and wink back. I was impressed with
his kindness. Especially knowing what I knew about his
past. It gave me hope that he would be understanding
when I told him my secret.

The server came back with Liam's credit card. He
signed for the meal, leaving a generous tip as always. "Are
you ready for our next stop?" He helped me out of my
chair and took my hand as we headed out.

"Can I have a hint?" I asked. I didn't want the day
to end.

Liam shook his head. "Nope. But I think you will
like it."

We drove for a while listening to the radio. Eventually
we pulled down a road and I saw where they were going.
"The zoo!! I love zoos. Well, the ones that actually care for
their animals properly."

~ LIAM ~

I couldn't help but smile at my animal loving girlfriend. "Then I think you'll really love this one."

Abigail was daffy as she practically jumped out of the car and quickly walked to the entrance. I just shook my head and laughed. I loved seeing Abigail so excited. For a brief moment, I wondered if our children would have her giddiness and pure joy. I shook the thought off quickly. It was too fast and too soon. But it was a nice daydream all the same. I caught up to Abigail at the ticket window. She already had her wallet out, ready to pay for tickets.

I put my hand over her wallet. "Hold on. I already have something planned." I gave the ticket agent my name and she pulled out two tickets and programs.

"If you have a seat to the right, your tour guide will be right out, Mr. Caffney."

Abigail gave me a look. "Tour guide?"

I nodded.

"You got us a private tour of the zoo?"

I nodded again and smiled.

Abigail hugged me and gave me a kiss. "You are just full of surprises, aren't you Mr. Caffney?"

I pulled Abigail in for a long lingering kiss. "That I am love, that I am."

Our guide cleared his throat, breaking us apart. "Mr. Caffney, hi, I'm Jeff. I'll be your tour guide this afternoon."

"Hi Jeff, please call me Liam and this is my girlfriend, Abi."

Abigail waved. "Hello."

Jeff gave her an odd look before quickly recovering and giving her a smile. "Shall we get started?"

Abigail sighed and grabbed my hand as we followed Jeff. Her sigh and his look were gnawing at me. I slowed, letting Jeff get several feet ahead of us. "What's wrong Abi?"

She shook her head but said nothing.

"Tell me. I can't try and help if I don't know what's wrong. I noticed Jeff and that look he tried to hide."

"It's nothing really. I've dealt with looks like Jeff gave me all of my life. I'm used to it, but it doesn't mean I don't get tired of it. It's the typical *'wow you're fat and why does this good looking skinny guy have you as girlfriend? Couldn't he do any better?'* I just choose to ignore it. Abigail shook her shoulders like she was shaking off a bad vibe. "I'm having too good of a day with you to let some close-minded idiot ruin it."

I kissed her hand. "Stay here a minute will you?"

"Liam"

I squeezed her hand. "Trust me, it'll just be a minute." I walked over to Jeff who had since turned around and was waiting for us. "Do you have a problem with my girlfriend, young Jeffrey?"

"Uh no, no sir." Jeff stuttered.

"Then what was that look you gave her? Don't think we didn't notice." I gave him one of my best '*I am better than you, because I'm on tv*' smiles.

"I'm sorry sir, but she just looks too heavy to do the zipline. We have weight limits, you know."

"I'm not debating that. I am however questioning your deduction that my girlfriend is simply too heavy. You have no idea what she weighs as you have not even bothered to ask her. Instead you are being a coward and talking to me about it."

"But you're the one who booked the activity sir."

"And *she* is the one you have the question about, Jeff. Do you have a problem with her, Jeff?"

"No of course not I—" Jeff looked over my shoulder and gulped. I looked over and saw Abigail was walking towards us.

I put my hand on Jeff's shoulder. "How about this, Jeffrey. Why don't you run along and get your manager for me? I'd like to have a word with them."

"I just, of course sir. I'll be right back."

Abigail grabbed my hand as she approached and watched Jeff scurry off. "Where is he going?"

"To get his manager."

"Liam, it's fine really, I'm used to people like him."

"Well, I'm not, and you shouldn't have to be." I could see Jeff and his manager approaching us. I gave Abigail's hand a squeeze. "I'll be right back, Abi.

I walked over to Jeff and his manager, a tall woman

with a bun in her hair and glasses around her neck. She reminded me of Abigail's principal. I had seen pictures of almost everyone Abigail worked with. All that was missing was a pencil stuck somewhere in her hair, and her being black of course.

I watched as the interaction between Liam and the manager went down. Jeff was there looking down while he shuffled his feet. The sight made me cringe a little. But if I really thought about it, there was a similarity to me getting used to fans interrupting our time and him getting used to me being fat shamed or ostracized because of my weight. There was a learning curve for both of us.

Liam walked back to me with a smile on his face. "We will have a new guide shortly. And a new first stop."

"I appreciate what you did Liam, but you really didn't need to. I can handle myself."

Liam wrapped me in a hug. "I know but let me be your knight in shining armor just this once."

I stroked his cheek and gave him a kiss. "Always."

A new guide named Mindy came over with a big smile on her face. "Hi Mr. Caffney! I'm Mindy and I'll be your guide." She shook his hand and then extended it to me. "And you are?"

"I'm Abi, nice to meet you."

"The pleasure is all mine, Abi. So, I've been told ziplining is out, but are you two ready for the experience of a lifetime?" Mindy had more zeal than I thought was necessary, but I loved her enthusiasm.

"Before we begin, can I just say I am a huge fan of yours, Mr. Caffney!" Mindy looked over her shoulder to see if her boss was around. "I know I shouldn't fangirl out on you, but I just had to say something. You are my absolute favorite."

Liam smiled "Please call me Liam. And I am honored that I am your favorite. Would you like a picture?"

"Well, I really shouldn't—"

"Aw come now, we're friends and all." Liam put his arm around Mindy. "Now hand Abi your phone so we can capture this moment. I know you must have it in a back or side pocket."

Mindy blushed as she took her phone out of her back pocket and handed it to me.

"Alright, get nice and close!" I chirped.

Liam winked at me as he put both arms around Mindy and pulled her into a tight hug. I took several pictures, the last was the best when Liam planted a kiss on Mindy's cheek. Her face was priceless and I had caught it on camera. I handed Mindy back her camera.

"Thank you so much. Shall we get started?"

"We'll follow your lead," Liam said.

I pulled his hand, holding him back as Mindy started walking towards our golf cart. "Did you book us to go ziplining?"

Liam nodded. "But Jeff seemed to have a problem with the idea, so I set something else up with Mindy. Something better." He kissed me, ending the conversation as he gently pulled me to catch up with Mindy. I decided to let it go and enjoy the day with Liam.

Mindy gave us an amazing tour taking us to all the popular animal spots as well as some of her favorite less known hidden gems around the zoo. We traveled mostly by golf cart but walked when she took us to the back section where only employees were allowed. I had a sneaky feeling we had carte blanche to go anywhere we wanted after Liam's little talk with the hospitality manager.

So far, feeding the giraffes has been my favorite part of the day. That was until we reached our last stop. Mindy pulled the cart around the back of the big cat enclosure. She took us through a building and down a hallway to a big empty room. It reminded me of a training room of sorts. I could see some balls in the corner and there were blankets and a table that had some bins on them. Mindy led us over to a little sitting area that was off to the side but still in the middle of the room.

"Please have a seat here. I'll be right back." Mindy quickly left the room.

"Do you know what she's doing?"

Liam smiled and shrugged.

"You do know! Tell me!" I poked his side making him laugh as he squirmed out of my reach.

"All I'll say is that it's your last surprise of the day. But who knows what tomorrow holds."

"You're going to spoil me the whole time I'm here, aren't you?" I chuckled.

"Absolutely! That way you'll want to come back sooner rather than later." Liam gave me a wink.

Mindy came back in with a zookeeper who was holding

a lion cub. "Liam mentioned to my boss how much you loved animals. That you volunteer at a shelter. He thought you might want to give this little girl a nice cuddle. Her name is Nyla."

"Nyla, really?" Liam asked with a raised eyebrow.

The zookeeper nodded. "We had a contest on our website. Nyla was the overwhelming winner. Second was the name Beatrice."

I let out a loud laugh, but quickly stopped. Clearly the zookeeper didn't get it. But Mindy did. Mindy shrugged. "I may have suggested a name or two to a few people who voted."

"It's perfect." Liam smiled as the zookeeper put the cub in his arms. He gave it a good hug before handing her off to me.

~ LIAM ~

I watched as unadulterated bliss swept across Abigail's face. She cuddled the cub right to her face and heard it purr. Her eyes welled up with tears.

"Hello little one. Aren't you a sight to behold?"

It was obvious that to Abigail everyone else in the room ceased to exist as she had a moment with little Nyla. I took out my phone and snapped picture after picture and Abigail was completely oblivious. After ten minutes the zookeeper had to take Nyla back to her mother. It was hard for Abigail to let sweet Nyla go.

"Thank you so much, that was better than I ever could have imagined." Abigail gushed as she handed Nyla back to the keeper.

"I hope you and Liam had a great tour today. I really enjoyed showing you around. I can take you back to the entrance." Mindy guided us back to the golf cart.

"Thank you Mindy. You've been a great tour guide," I said as we sat back down in the golf cart.

Once back at the entrance I took a picture of the three

of us. One with my phone and then another with Mindy's.
I held out a tip for Mindy. "You made our day Mindy,
thank you so much."

"Oh thank you, but I can't. It's against policy and —"

I took the money, put it in Mindy's palm and folded
her fingers over it. "I insist."

Mindy looked around to make sure there were no
supervisors or managers around. "Thanks! And again it
was great meeting you. Thank you for the pictures. And
you too Abi. I had a blast."

We waved goodbye to Mindy, then walked back to the
car, hand in hand, swinging our arms. It had been a very
very good day.

~ ABIGAIL ~

The next two days were much the same for us, sensual morning sex followed by visiting different areas of Toronto that Liam wanted to share with me. He had surprises of some kind almost every day. My week was going by so fast and my phone was quickly filling up with photos. I was excited to show them all to Tess when I returned home. There was so much to tell her. We had texted a couple of times, and had one brief phone call when Liam was at work, but I really wanted to center all my attention on him.

As usual, I was up first. I gave Liam a kiss on the forehead and headed to the kitchen to start breakfast. I felt like making ricotta pancakes. I was pretty sure he had all the ingredients.

I looked in the refrigerator and was very happy to find some fresh ricotta from the Marketplace we had gone to the day before. I was on my tiptoes reaching for a mixing bowl when I felt Liam and his hardness grab me from behind. I smiled to myself. I loved this little ritual of being drawn back to bed for some playtime before we officially started our day.

Liam kissed my neck reaching his hands underneath my sleep shirt so he could play with my breasts and nipples. "Good morning, love," he whispered in my ear before he licked it. "I had a great dream about you." He kissed my neck as his hands roamed down my thighs and between my legs, and slowly stroked my slit. I got wetter at every touch.

"Really?" I gasped as he tweaked my nipple, then bit my neck. "Tell me about it."

Hooking my panties under his thumbs he pulled them down. "Let me show you instead." He wedged his legs between mine and guided me down so I was bent over the counter and entered me from behind.

I grabbed at the counter as I moaned, "Oh fuck." I loved the way he felt inside me. He made my entire body hum and vibrate with each thrust. I bit my lip to muffle my moans.

Liam chuckled. He knew how loud I could get. What he could bring out of me. "It's okay love, I have thick walls."

That's all I needed. I started to moan loudly which only set Liam off. He enjoyed making me moan, and the louder the better. It felt like his cock got even harder as my moans grew. Liam drilled me and I bent over even further, giving him more access, wanting him to go deeper. He pulled at my braids wrapping them around his hand. "That's right love, open up to me."

"I'm yours Liam, only yours," I cried.

"That's my good, good girl." Liam kissed and nipped at my back between thrusts. It wasn't long before my walls began to quiver as my breath quickened and turned to gasps. My walls clamped down around his cock as I climaxed and yelled his name. Two more thrusts and he released deep inside me. He slumped onto my back. We were both out of breath but very happy.

Liam caressed my back as he pulled out and looked at the ingredients on the counter. "Oh! Were you going to make ricotta pancakes?"

"I was, but I got a little distracted." I smiled as I turned to finally face him. "Would you still like some?"

"Yes please." Liam batted his lush green eyes at me. "Shower with me first?" He leaned in, claiming my lips as his.

I could feel my body begin to tingle again. I couldn't get enough of him. I grabbed his ass thrusting towards me.

Liam laughed. "I'll take that as a yes." He grabbed my hand and ran me to the bathroom.

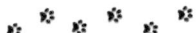

I was eventually able to make some ricotta pancakes which we ate with blueberries and some Canadian pure maple syrup. I was cleaning up the dishes when Liam came out of the living room with a picnic basket and began rooting through the pantry and refrigerator.

"Are we going on a picnic today?"

"Yes! There is a special spot in High Park I want to take you to. I get some of my best meditation done there. You should bring a notebook. You might get inspired."

I couldn't help but smile. Liam was really encouraging me to write more. I was surprised with how much I had written on this trip already. "I'll bring my notebook if you

bring your camera. You never know what might inspire
you."

Liam kissed my cheek as he playfully smacked my ass.
"I'm pretty sure I know what my inspiration will be today."
He finished packing the basket while I finished cleaning
up and getting ready. Thirty minutes later we were on our
way to High Park. The parking lot was about half full by
the time we got there.I didn't know how big the park actually was, and I was worried it might be crowded.

I had no need to worry, the park was huge. Liam led
the way to his favorite spot. It was pretty secluded in
comparison to many of the other wide open spaces in
the park. This section had a lot of trees clumped
together almost forming a grove of sorts with little
pocket inlets. Some had people in them lounging about.
Others had no one but the sun and some squirrels. Liam
seemed to have a favorite grove set back a little farther
from the others. No one was there. He laid out the big
blanket he had brought along with two pillows that I had
never seen him put in the car. He then rooted around for
some drinks.

"Where did those come from? I asked as I pointed to
the pillows.

"Ah! Those are my park pillows. I keep them in my car
at all times."

"You have park pillows? No decorative pillows on your
bed, but park pillows in your car." I laughed.

"Of course! Doesn't everybody?" He winked and
handed me a drink as he sat down.

I sat down next to him. "This place really is beautiful,
thank you for bringing me here."

Liam began playing with my braids. "I love running

your braids through my fingers. It's very soothing, almost zen-like."

"I feel the same way about your curls."

"Are you having a good trip, Abi?"

I closed my eyes, nodding. "I'm having a wonderful time. It makes me dream."

"Dream about what?" Liam stroked my cheek.

I looked into his eyes. "Traveling the world with you. Seeing places I've never seen, never been to, and sharing that all with you."

"Should we quit our jobs and travel the world?"

I grinned. "I was thinking something a little less drastic. Maybe after next season, season five, and at the end of my school year, we can spend the summer together? They almost lineup, right?"

"That sounds lovely." Liam leaned in, giving me a kiss.

"Maybe start in Ireland and go from there?"

Liam pulled me up into his arms pressing his soft lips against my plump ones. He looked into my eyes. "I love you." He kissed me again.

I didn't know what took my breath away more, his words, or his kiss. I melted into the kiss, reaching to hold his hand. I pulled back so I could look him in the eye. "I love you too."

Liam leaned against a tree and I nestled into his arms. I sighed, letting out a big breath, feeling very content. This feeling is what I had wanted my whole life and didn't realize I'd been holding my breath waiting for it to arrive.

We spent the afternoon in the park. I got some writing done. Liam took out his camera and got what he hoped were some great nature shots. We munched on the treats Liam had packed in the basket and shared a brief nap lulled to sleep by the breeze from the trees. The sun was beginning to set by the time we started packing up.

"We have dinner at my friend Ted's house. I want to shower and change before we go."

"Me too," I agreed. I stood and helped collect our belongings.

Liam pulled me into a hug. "Shower together?" he asked as he kissed me.

Although I would never tire of his kisses I twirled my way out of his arms. "If we do that, we'll be late and you know it, so no."

Liam pretended to pout. I took his face in my hands and gave him a kiss. "I'll make it up to you when we get home. I promise."

Liam couldn't help but smile. "It's home now, is it?"

"Maybe." I winked and headed back down the path to the car.

~ ABIGAIL ~

I looked at myself in Liam's full length mirror. My gray off the shoulder sweater hugged me just right and the scoop neckline showed off the gold necklace Liam had given me perfectly. My black jeans were a deep black so it was a lovely contrast. My black boots finished off the look nicely.

I had already changed my outfit twice and was debating on trying on one more outfit when Liam walked in. He looked amazing in his jeans and button down maroon shirt. The color played well with his eyes, making them even greener.

"You look lovely Abi."

I turned slowly one more time. "Are you sure? I can change into something else."

"We aren't going to meet the queen, just dinner with friends," Liam joked. He saw the look of concern on my face. "Have I mentioned you look gorgeous?"

I looked in the mirror again. Liam was right, I did look gorgeous. "Okay, I think I'm ready. Wait! Just need some lipstick." I ran back into the bathroom to get my favorite lipstick out of my makeup bag. I applied it while looking in the bathroom mirror, puckering my lips and giving myself a wink. Now I was truly ready. Liam held the door open for me, giving me a peck on the cheek as we headed out.

I looked out the window as we drove. "Ted lives in the suburbs?"

"Yes, he and his girlfriend bought a house about a year and a half ago. You're going to love Connie. I have a feeling the two of you are going to get along really well. The show brought them together, you know?"

I just nodded. Now that Liam knew I had started watching the show, I felt it would be fine to make a comment about it. "He does a good job on the show. You two work well together. At least that's what comes across on screen."

Liam reached for my hand and gave it a squeeze. "Thanks love. We have a good time together, hit it off right away."

As we pulled into the driveway Ted opened the door and waved. "Welcome friends!"

Liam and I got out of the car and headed up the walk. Liam and Ted shared the standard bro hug. Then Ted reached out and pulled me into a hug. "Abi! It's grand to see you again. This guy just wouldn't shut up about you after you left the set the other day!"

I returned the hug. "Well, I hope it's all good."

"Oh yes! But not too good!" Ted winked.

"Ted! Stop standing in the doorway and invite them in!" Connie called from the living room. She was setting down a final plate of hors d'oeuvres when we came in and sat down.

"Connie, this is the infamous Abi," Ted introduced me.

"It's so nice to meet you." She shook my hand.

"So I'm infamous now?" I looked over at Liam. He just shrugged and smiled

"Don't worry, it's a good thing." Connie chuckled. "Especially with this one over here." She reached out her arms to Liam. "Come give me a hug." Connie hugged him and then turned back to me. "What can I get you to drink? Wine? I've got red and white."

"I'd love some red." Liam was right. I already could tell I like Connie.

"I'll take red too please." Liam put his arm around me.

"I think it'll be red all around hun." Ted nodded.

"No problem, Abi, would you mind helping me?" Connie asked.

"Of course not." I stood up and followed Connie into the kitchen.

"Can you get the wine opener? It's in the drawer on your left," Connie asked as she pulled the wine glasses out of the cabinet.

I found it quickly and handed it to Connie. "You have a lovely kitchen. I wish mine was this nice, I wish mine was this size!"

"Apartment kitchen?"

I nodded. "How did you know?"

"I used to wish the same thing until we got this house."

"Oh, so you live here year round? Not just when they are filming?"

Connie nodded. "I'm a native. I met Ted here on his

last show. I actually helped him find his apartment while filming."

"Real estate agent?" I asked.

"Yup!" Connie opened the wine, handing the cork to me. "I helped Ted find his place like I mentioned and then helped a bunch of his other cast mates. That show only lasted a season and a half. They canceled it mid-season. When he came back for *EverMorphs,* he called me again and brought half of his cast with him. I somehow became the unofficial realtor of *The Ever-Morphs.* I'm not complaining, mind you. It's been quite the gift. And I got a great possible husband out of the deal." She nodded her head towards the laughter coming from the living room.

"Really? Are you expecting a ring soon?" I whispered.

Connie smiled. "I'd like to think so. I'm kind of getting a feeling off of Teddy lately. He'll deny it of course. But a woman knows."

"I'm so happy for you! That's exciting!"

"What's exciting?" Ted asked as he came in for more shrimp cocktail sauce.

Looking at Connie I gave a slight nod. "My first trip to Toronto. It's all been so exciting."

Ted looked back and forth between the two of us. "For some reason, I don't believe you." He turned his head towards the living room. "Liam! I think our girls are getting along too well! This could be a problem." He gave a wink to Connie and refilled the cocktail sauce. I just shook my head. Another winker. Was everyone on the show winkers? Connie handed me two glasses, she grabbed the other two, and the three of us headed back into the living room.

"What's this I hear? Are the ladies getting into trouble already?" Liam chided.

I gave Liam a glass of wine. "Just telling secrets."

"Ack! Teddy, we're doomed! They are already sharing secrets!" Liam joked.

"And they are *really* juicy!" Connie teased.

"Abi! Did you tell her about the time we did the thing and how it made you—"

I gave Liam's arm a playful slap. "Oh my god no! Stop talking!"

We all started to laugh.

"And on that note I think dinner is ready. Ted, show them to the dining room and I'll get the food." Connie left to get the meal out of the oven.

"Yes dear," Ted replied in a very sing-song voice. He showed us into the dining room. Connie had made beautiful place cards in the shape of different kinds of trees. Each one had individual leaves on the branches and our names were spelled out in the roots.

Liam gave a long whistle as he picked it up and looked at the details. "Teddy, you weren't kidding when you said she was in a decorating mood."

I nodded in agreement. "These are gorgeous." I noticed the extra place setting, with the name Ryan on it. "Are we waiting on someone?"

"Oh, my uncle was supposed to join us. He's in town on business but got held up. He might be here for dessert."

Connie came in before I could say anything else and put a large roast beef platter on the table. It was surrounded by roasted carrots and potatoes. "Dinner is served. Oops! Almost forgot the rolls. I'll be right back." Connie dashed into the kitchen and was back in a moment with a dish of hot rolls. I could see the steam rolling off of them. "Bon Appetit!" Connie took her seat. "Ted, will you do the honors?"

Ted cut up the roast beef as we handed him our plates for him to put some slices on. The rest of the food was passed around and everyone took what they wanted. For a few minutes all I could hear was the sound of silverware on plates and all of us enjoying our food.

"This is just delicious Connie. I need this recipe please." I said between bites.

"Thank you. I'd be happy to share it with you. So Abi, tell me, how did you meet Liam?"

I took a sip of my wine. "I would have thought he told you by now."

Connie nodded. "Oh, he did, but you know men, they never give good details."

"Hey, I take offense." Liam put his hand to his chest.

I reached over and squeezed his hand. "Well, to be honest, my boss foisted Liam on me."

"Foisted?" Connie cocked her head to the side. "Do tell, I want details."

"I volunteer at an animal shelter." I started.

"Ah! So that's where he got the kitten from!"

I nodded. "Yes, for some reason Liam agreed to help us out with our annual adoption and fundraising event. In the past we've had celebrities come in and help raise money but no one of Liam's status before."

Liam smiled. "Did you hear that Ted? I'm of a certain status."

"Don't let your head swell mate. I'm still before you on the call sheet."

"Ouch! Right through the heart man!"

"Anyway, my boss Steve, didn't want to team Liam up with one of our younger volunteers because he was afraid they would go fan crazy, and not be able to accomplish the task at hand."

"Hmm, you make fan sound like a four letter word." Connie noted.

"So," Liam interrupted, "they placed me with a seasoned professional. And the rest is history."

"A non-fan, interesting," Connie commented.

"Is it really that interesting? I mean most fans are-"

"Careful, love" Liam interjected. "Connie is a fan."

"Really?" That made me feel much better. "You're an *EverMorph* fan?"

"Not just *EverMorph*. I was a fan of Ted before he even got that job. I loved him way back when he was on *Space Riders*."

Ted groaned. "An experience I wish I could forget, but *someone* owns the box set!"

"You bet your sweet bippy I do! It's even signed."

"Sorry Connie, Teddy's signature doesn't count." Liam laughed.

"Oh no, I have the entire cast, not just my Teddy." Connie smiled. I could tell it was a great accomplishment for her. Connie was proud to be a fan and it fascinated me.

"Dessert anyone? I made strawberry shortcake." Connie smiled as she got up and started to clear the plates.

"Let me help you Connie." I offered.

"Scotch?" Ted asked Liam.

Liam nodded. "After you." They headed back to the living room.

In the kitchen I began to probe Connie a little more.

"So you were always a fan of Ted's work? Did that worry you at all about what he would think of you?"

"What do you mean?"

"Sometimes fans don't have the best reputation. I was wondering if it made Ted hesitant to get to know you. Or you know him?"

Connie thought about it for a moment. "I don't really think so. It's not like we met at a fan convention or anything. I was just the lucky realtor who was in the office when he walked in."

"So how did he know you were a fan?"

"Oh I told him. Once I had arranged his apartment, and the lease was signed, I told him and then asked him out." Connie smiled.

"And he was just like sure?" I couldn't believe what I was hearing.

Connie laughed. "Oh god no! He was hesitant at first. So we just had coffee, and then another coffee, and then a walk, and then lunch, and so on and so on. Eventually we got to where we are now."

"So he was cautious because you were a fan, are a fan." It confirmed my beliefs on the matter.

Connie shrugged. "Maybe. But now, I think he thinks it's cute that I'm a fan of him and his work. Actually I even have a username dedicated to him."

"You mean like for your email or something?" I inquired.

Connie reached for her phone. "Let me show you something." Connie pulled up a blog page. "I follow Ted's current show with a bunch of other fans. We comment and speculate on characters. It's a lot of fun. You make up a name to go with your profile. Usually it relates to the show, I guess you could use your own name if you wanted to. But I don't know anyone that does. I go by *IFollowFlint*. This particular show blog is run by *Eternally Evers*."

I did my best not to show any emotion. "May I take a look?"

"Sure." Connie handed me her phone. I scrolled through it. I took a deep breath and let it out slowly trying not to panic. Maybe my first step could be to confide in Connie. I knew I had just met her, but if anyone would understand, it would be her.

"She's actually quite funny and very insightful about the show. You should make a profile and follow her! We could have some great fun." Connie tried to convince me.

I gave Connie her phone back. "Connie, can I tell you something? But you have to promise not to tell Liam or Ted."

I could see the wheels turning in her head. "Abigail -"

"Abi, please."

Connie nodded. "Abi, from the moment you walked in the door I knew you would be around for a long time. I see the way Liam's face lights up when he talks about you. And now that you are here it is even brighter. After his last girlfriend, and I use that term loosely. I promised to go all big sister on anyone else who came into his life. No more crazy bitches. But you, you're the real deal. I'm really happy that Liam has some light and love back in his life, and I will do anything to help preserve that. He's family, I don't know Abi, I can't keep—"

"I'm *Etertnally Evers*, the blog is mine!" I blurted out.

"Blog! Do people still do those? Who has a blog? What's an *Eternally Evers*?" A tall man who resembled Ted in the eyes came into the kitchen. "I heard there was some strawberry shortcake in here."

"Uncle Ryan! I'm so glad you made it!" Connie gave Ryan a big hug. "I'd like you to meet Liam's girlfriend, Abi. Abi, this is Ted's uncle, Ryan Motlen."

Ryan stuck out his hand and gave me his show smile. "Have we met before?"

~ ABIGAIL ~

Liam and Ted came into the kitchen.

"See Teddy, I told you the party was in here."

"We were just coming out with dessert." I tried to pull myself together.

"I think they were telling more secrets. What do you think Liam?" Ted joked.

Liam nodded. "Trouble, with a capital T."

"Uncle Ryan, I see you met Abi?"

Ryan nodded. "Yes, as a matter of fact I was just asking her if we had met before." Ryan took a good look at me. "You just look so familiar to me, but I can't place you. Could I have met you at a fan event?"

"No, not my Abi, she's not much for fandoms." Liam put his arm around me, kissing the side of my head.

I moved into him. I needed to feel safe. I couldn't believe who was standing in front of me. The man who turned "*fan*" into a four letter word for me. The man who had shattered me at seventeen was Ted's uncle. "May I use your restroom please."

"Sure, it's down the hall to your left." Connie pointed it out.

I nodded. "Excuse me please." I quickly walked down the hallway, and gently closed the bathroom door behind me. I took several deep breaths and ran some cold water over my hands, hoping it would calm my nerves. I willed myself not to cry. Looking in the mirror, I gave myself a talking to. "The past is the past. You leave Ryan Motlen there. You can do this. Have a nice dessert, and the minute you get home, you sit down and tell Liam everything." I nodded, resolved with a plan. I took a few more minutes to collect myself. I gave a final nod to the mirror, put a smile on my face and headed out of the bathroom. I heard voices in the living room and headed in that direction.

"They say everything lasts forever on the internet, no matter how you try to delete it." Ryan confirmed. "I knew she was familiar, and it was gonna gnaw at my bones until I figured it out." He looked up and saw me staring at them all huddled around Ted's laptop. Ryan turned the laptop around to show me something I hadn't seen in fifteen years. It was the video of my outburst at Sci-Con. It was old and a little fuzzy but there was no doubt it was me. I couldn't move or speak.

Ryan looked up at me. "I owe you an apology, Abi. I was a selfish, self-absorbed son of a bitch back then. Way too big for my britches, and very unappreciative." Ryan shook his head and chuckled. "I actually got in a hot bit of trouble for that and so did my castmate if I recall! And some not too pretty hefty fines from the show. It was an eye opener for sure."

I looked at Liam. He had a look on his face I had never seen. It was one of heartbreak, anger and disappointment.

Ryan continued, oblivious to the tension that was building in the room. "Let me make it up to you. It was a shame that you took your blog down after that. I know because I checked, and what little I did read that day was really quite brilliant. It had to be, to stick in this old noodle for so long. Maybe with the reboot of the show, you could take up the mantle again. It would be great PR for the show. And now that I have an inside track to you, I'm sure we could make something real good together."

I went to sit down, but not next to Liam. I couldn't be that close to him right now. "Well, I-"

Ryan kept yapping his mouth. "You really were a die-hard *Lost Continent* fan. What about *The EverMorphs*? Do you have a blog for that too? Let's take a look." Ryan looked down at the laptop.

Ted gently closed it, shaking his head. He got up to put it in the study where it belonged.

"Hey, Uncle Ryan, how about we skip that and have some dessert? Would anyone like coffee or tea to go with theirs? The whip cream is homemade." Connie started to hand out plates of dessert.

~ LIAM ~

Ted came back into the room and looked at me. "Hey mate, will you help me get some more coffee and tea? I can't handle all of it without breaking something. And Connie will kill me if it's one of her favorite mugs or god forbid a teacup." He pretended to shake in his shoes.

I nodded as I got up. I turned to Connie. "Fear not Connie. I'll make sure your cupware stays intact." I bowed and headed into the kitchen.

Ted already had the tea kettle on and the coffee brewing. He pulled out a chair for me to sit. "That was unexpected."

"Aye, you could knock me over with a feather right now."

"How are you doing there?" Ted handed me a shot. I had no idea where it came from, but I was grateful.

I downed the shot, shrugged and shook my head. "She lied."

"Did she though? I mean that was fifteen years ago.

She wasn't even an adult then. And trust me, from the stories my mom told me about my uncle back in the day, he and his co-stars weren't the nicest to their fans. Maybe get the full story before you make a judgment call."

"Doesn't matter. It is a non-negotiable. Ever since Siobhan I made it a hard rule."

Ted put his hand on my shoulder. "I know everything that happened between you and Siobhan. And I know it wrecked you. But does Abi know everything? Or anything really."

I threw my hands up. "Of course she does! She's a goddamn fan!"

Ted handed me another shot. "Shh, calm down man."

"Media truth and real truth are very different things. You know that. Abi is a catch and she lights you up. Give her the benefit of the doubt and hear her out."

I grabbed the teacups Ted handed me. "I don't know mate, I think it's the lying more than the being a fan thing. As if Siobhan wasn't enough , then came hurricane Bianca. You know the lies and deceptions I went through with both of them. Always the lies man."

"This is a lot I know, so maybe put it on the back burner for now and let's just have dessert and enjoy each other's company."

I nodded. "You're right. You're right. And now is not the time for it. Now is the time for tea."

"And coffee!" Ted held up the coffee mugs.

We walked back into the living room to find Ryan telling tales of his glory days on *Lost Continent*. Connie was being gracious and so was Abigail, but she looked like she was going to be sick. "And I'll be here filming a couple of episodes shortly after your men return to the set of *Ever-Morphs*! It'll be great!" Ryan smiled.

"It will be nice to see you more, Uncle Ryan."

"I'm hoping your girl here will help me find the perfect bachelor pad when the time comes. No hotel for me. I want my space."

Connie nodded. "Of course Uncle Ryan, not a problem."

Dessert continued to be awkward as both Abigail and I were having trouble keeping up our end of the conversations. Connie tried her best, knowing the shit was going to hit the fan eventually. I know she hoped it would wait until after the evening was over.

Ryan had to feel the tension, but I'm sure he had no clue what it was for. From what I knew about Ryan he always tried to liven things up a bit. "So, how is everything going at *EverMorphs*? Only two more episodes to film right?"

Ted nodded. "Two more before a nice break until next season begins filming."

"What? No project in between? Connie, you're not turning my nephew into a slacker, are you?"

"Hey! Watch it Uncle! I'm choosing not to do anything this break. I have some other plans that shall not be talked about at the moment."

Ryan shrugged. "I'll say no more." He pulled out his phone, looking for something.

"Ted told me you visited the set earlier in the week. Did you have a good time? Meet anybody?" Connie asked.

Abigail nodded as she finished her bite of strawberry shortcake. "Yes, I mean I didn't get to see much and I had to sign an NDA, but it was exciting watching Liam while he filmed. I wasn't even paying attention to the storyline. I was just watching everyone perform. It was wonderful, almost magical."

Ryan chuckled, "Sounds like a true fan to me. Liam, do you know what an EternallyEvers is?"

I shook my head. "I have no idea what that is."

"The ladies were talking about it when I came in. Apparently, your lovely girl is one."

"Uncle Ryan, you misunderstood what we were talking about." Connie tried to defuse the situation before it got any worse.

I looked at Abigail. "Do you know what he is talking about?"

Before Abigail could say anything , Ryan handed me his phone. "See this is EternallyEvers, or at least the person who runs what looks like a website blog all about your show! It's called *And That's All I Have to Say About That.*" Ryan turned to Abigail and smiled. "So you do have another blog. That's terrific. It means you haven't gotten rusty. We really do need to have a talk about you doing one for the reboot. I'm sure there would be a nice salary in it for you."

Abigail looked dumbfounded. So she just remained silent.

"Sorry Ryan, this isn't Abi's blog. She doesn't have one." I grabbed her hands and gave it a reassuring squeeze. Even if I was upset with her, the look on her face made me reach out.

"Huh, I could have sworn I heard her tell Connie that she was Eternally Evers." He turned to Connie. "Isn't that what she said to you, Connie?"

Connie had a bad poker face. She shook her head, but

her facial expression clearly said yes. "As I said, you misunderstood. We were talking about a fan site, and fans in general, that's all."

Ryan looked back and forth between the ladies. Eventually he shrugged and took a sip of his coffee. "Oh well, I guess I was wrong. It's been known to happen from time to time." He chuckled as he took his phone back and took a bite of shortcake.

The whole time this conversation was going on I had been scrolling through the blog *And That's All I Have To Say About That! All Things EverMorph All the Time.* I had a feeling creeping into my gut and I didn't like it. I prayed he was wrong. I wanted to believe Abigail wouldn't lie about something this big. But I couldn't shake the feeling that my bubble was bursting. Ryan took his phone back

I gave a fake yawn. "I'm so sorry but I'm beat, and tomorrow is Abi's last full day, so I have one last big surprise planned for her."

Abigail stood up. "I had a wonderful time. I hope we get to spend more time together." She gave Connie and Ted a hug. "And thank you for the apology, Ryan." Abigail grabbed her purse and headed to the door.

I said my goodbyes and followed her out.

~ LIAM ~

The ride home was quiet. Halfway home I broke the silence. "Are you EterntallyEvers? Is that your blog? Are you a fan of the show? Of me?" I couldn't look at Abigail when I asked. I kept my eyes glued to the road.

I felt Abigail turn to me, I knew she could see the strained look on my face. Was she going to lie to me? Her long silence made me think she was actually debating between telling me the truth or making up more lies. I pursed my lips and sat in silence waiting for her answer.

Finally Abigail took a deep breath and let it out. I could feel her eyes boring into my head, but I refused to even glance at her. "Yes, it's my blog. I am EterntallyEvers."

I swallowed hard. A million thoughts went through my mind. I was angry and hurt and had so many questions. Most of all I felt betrayed and deceived.

"I'd like to explain it all to you if you'll let me." Abigail tried not to cry. "I didn't mean to lie, I just didn't want the stigma that went with being a fan of the show, of you. And honestly, I never thought what happened between us would actually happen. I just thought we would have a great time at the shelter, that would be the end of it and I would have a happy memory. I never imagined any of this. And then we had feelings, I felt like it was too late to tell you about my blog and have you understand, so I just omitted it." Abigail took a short breath and kept going. "I was planning on telling you everything on this trip I swear. Ryan just beat me to it. I'm not some crazy stalker fan, I know the difference between you and your characters, I never meant to take you for granted or deceive you. I just, I just didn't."

My knuckles grew white as I gripped the steering wheel, not even giving Abigail a side glance. She was waiting for me to say something. I kept quiet.

"Say something Liam, please. Ask me anything, I promise to give you an honest answer."

I gave her a quick look before concentrating on the road again. I reached my hand over and turned on the radio. I had nothing to say.

I opened the door forAbigail, letting her enter my apartment first. I immediately went to the kitchen to pour two glasses of wine. Aoife wound herself between my legs and purred. I picked her up cuddling her for a moment before making sure she had food and water. Once she was settled, I went into the living room. Abigail was sitting straight up on the couch clasping her hands together and trying to keep her breathing even.

I handed her a glass of wine. She gratefully took it.

"So you knew who I was right from the start. You knew all about *The EverMorphs*. And you have a blog about the show? How long have you had that?"

Abigail let out an audible gulp. "Almost four years. I started it after the third episode of the first season."

I went to the kitchen and grabbed the wine bottle and brought it back to the living room with me. I refilled my glass and drank half of it. I shut my eyes, bowed my head and counted to ten before looking up again. "You mentioned seeing *Keys*. Have you seen anything else?"

Abigail nodded. "I've seen the majority of your movies and television appearances. You're an extremely talented actor."

I sucked down the rest of the wine in my glass. "Thank you, I guess. Today you said you love me. Are you in love with me? Or are you in love with who you perceive as the celebrity me?"

Abigail turned, grabbed my hand in hers, and looked directly in my eyes. "I love you, Liam Matthew Caffney. I love your kindness and your humor, your compassion, and your intelligence. I love your eye for photography and how you bring the natural beauty out in every image. I love how you treat others, and the warmth in your heart. I love how you love me and make me laugh. And yes, I love your talent. But that is only such a small part of all that encompasses who you are. Please believe me when I say there are no words for how sorry I am that I wasn't completely upfront with you from the beginning."

I kissed her hand and leaned my cheek against it. Closing my eyes, I let myself just breathe. I loved this woman. She brought something out in me that hasn't surfaced in a long time. And in my core I knew I could trust her. "I believe you."

Abigail let out a sigh of relief. "You deserve to know the whole story about that video and why I feel the way I do about being a fan, and why I hid it from you." She looked down as she gulped the remainder of her wine.

I shook my head. My voice was steady but firm. "I saw enough to get the gist. And if I thought I missed something, uncle Ryan was pretty clear. But Abi, I need to know, is there anything else I should know? You aren't hiding anything else, are you? I need the truth. All of it. And I'll give you the same in return. If you have questions about Bianca or even Siobhan I will tell you. But I can't take the lies, Abi. We can work through anything. But not lies. I've had enough of that in relationships. I'm not doing that ever again."

"I promise there is nothing else."

I drew Abigail into my arms and kissed her. "Only honesty from now on, okay? I can't be with someone who lies to me."

"I promise, only honesty." She kissed me, wrapping her arms around me like she never wanted to let go. We stayed like that, holding on tight and giving delicate kisses until my phone rang. Begrudgingly I released myself from Abigail's arms to answer it. It was the studio. I got up and walked away to take the call.

~ ABIGAIL ~

I felt myself relax as Liam went to take his phone call. My body shook as I realized how close I had just come to losing him. I knew I loved him, but now I knew I didn't want to be without him, ever. All the cards had been laid on the table and we had survived. I shook my arms and legs out trying to release the pent up tension. A few minutes later Liam came back in, still on the phone and stared at me as he talked.

"Yes, so you have the winner of the contest. You want me to see their spring production? Yes, I can do that. Okay, what school am I going to again? That's in Connecticut? It's Odyssey High, home of the fighting blue sharks? And can you tell me why you picked that school? What put them over the top? Oh, their teacher makes homemade stickers for her students about *The EverMorphs*? Great, just email everything and I'll be there with bells on. Wouldn't want to disappoint my fans."

He looked at me, not just at me, but through me. He was beyond angry. "And I guess I'll wear something blue since they are the fighting blue sharks and all. Yes, okay thank you."

Liam hung up the phone and went to the bedroom. It wasn't long before he walked back to the living room with a duffle bag in his hand. I was sitting on the couch dumbfounded. "I'm going to Ted's for the night. I'll be back sometime tomorrow. Please watch over Aoife. Have a good night, Abi."

I tried to grab his arm to make him stay and talk. I had no idea why my school had won. I hadn't entered them in the contest. I thought about it, but that was before Liam. At this point, I didn't think he would believe me, but I had to try. "Liam, wait! Let's talk about this. I swear to you I did NOT enter my school. There must be some mistake."

Liam pulled his arm away. "But you blogged about it. I saw it. So why shouldn't I believe that you entered? It took all of five minutes for another lie to come out. You could have just told me when I asked. But no, you had to go and hide it. You had to be a sneaky little bitch just like Siobhan and you tried to make me the fool just like Bianca. You're all such conniving little bitches.

"Liam, that's not fair! Don't compare me to them. This is all a misunderstanding!"

"You should see if you can change your flight. It would be best for you to leave as soon as possible. I'll pay the difference. I'll see you in a month for your students' performance." With that, Liam walked out the door.

I crumbled to the floor and cried. Aoife came and climbed on my lap. She gave me sweet kitty kisses trying to cheer me up. It only made me cry harder. Holding Aoife I found my phone and called Tess.

"Tess, I'm headed to the airport. Can you come pick

me up when I land? No, I don't know what airline or even what airport yet. I'm just going to get the first flight out I can. I'll explain it all when I see you. But keep your phone close. Please? Thanks Tess, I don't know what I'd do without you. I'll call you when I have flight information."

I went to the bedroom and started packing. I sat on the bed and the tears started again as I picked up a picture of us at the zoo with little Nyla. Liam had blown up one of the photos and gotten it framed. I hadn't realized how many souvenirs I had picked up on this trip until I tried packing. As I finished up Aoife jumped on the bed. I scooped her ups and laid down on the bed with her. The fetal position was all I could handle.

I must have fallen asleep. I woke up thinking the night had been a bad dream. But it was pitch black and I quickly remembered it wasn't. I grabbed a piece of paper and started to write Liam a note. I tried to explain everything. But the more I wrote the more angry I became. I wasn't a conniving bitch. I was nothing like Siobhan or Bianca and he knew that. He had sunk to name calling to try and hurt me. I swore to him I wouldn't lie to him and he wouldn't give me the benefit of the doubt. He said he loved me but he wouldn't even hear me out. I ripped the note in half and left it on the bed. I refreshed Aoife's food and water. I then scooped out her little box before grabbing her for some goodbye cuddles. I left the light in the bedroom on, gave Aoife one last snuggle then grabbed my bag and waited outside for my uber to take me to the airport.

~ LIAM ~

Ryan's car wasn't there when I arrived at Ted's place. I was very glad for that. I didn't feel up to facing the man who blew up my world in a matter of minutes. I knocked on the door. Connie was quick to open it. I could tell by the look on her face she had a feeling something like this might be how the night ended. She gave me a hug.

"Can I crash in your spare room?" I let out a loud sigh.

"Of course, come on in. Ted has some scotch in his office already waiting for you."

I snorted. "So, you were expecting me."

Connie shrugged. "I also have wine in the kitchen. Just in case it was Abi.

My face hardened at the sound of her name. "In the office you said?"

Connie nodded and I headed towards the office. She was a smart and intuitive woman. I heard her sigh as the lock clicked shut and the room dim as she turned off the lights. She was smart enough to know to head to bed by herself. She knew Ted and I would be up for a while talking. Or drinking, Or drinking and talking.

I woke up to the smell of bacon and coffee, and a blistering headache. I stretched, reaching over my head for Aoife. It was a knee jerk reaction by this point. I sighed when I realized she couldn't possibly be there. I got up and rambled into the kitchen to find Connie at the griddle. She handed me a cup of coffee before flipping the bacon. "How did you sleep?"

I took several sips of coffee then reached for the milk and sugar on the table. "I slept so-so."

"You know she loves you and didn't mean to hurt you right?" She handed me a stack of pancakes.

"And you know this from all the time you spent together being best friends, is that it?"

"Hey! Don't be snarky. She's a good person and you know it. She felt bad about keeping such a big secret from you. I could tell by the conversation we had. I could have gotten more but Ryan walked in."

"Gah! Ryan, he literally blew up my world last night. That guy is a peach!"

"Don't blame the messenger. Although he didn't really know what he was blowing up. He also didn't know when to shut the hell up."

"I completely agree with that!" Ted walked into the kitchen. "Sorry about all of that, Liam."

"Not your fault mate."

Connie placed plates of food on the table. All perfect hangover dishes. "I hate to mention it, but did you just leave Abi at your apartment? Have you talked to her since you got here?"

I shook my head.

"Liam! Don't be a tool. Call her right now. Or no more coffee for you!" Ted pulled my coffee cup away from me.

"Fine! Fine!" I got up to make the call, but grabbed a pancake and a piece of bacon before heading to the next room. I called but her phone went straight to voicemail. I called three times and got her voicemail every time. I came back into the kitchen and started eating my breakfast.

Connie looked from me to Ted and back again. "Well?!"

"I got her voice mail. Three times." I shrugged,

"So, that's it? You're done?"

I put down my fork and wiped my mouth. "I have no idea what anything means at the moment."

"But you still love her?"

I sighed. "Of course I do. I just need to figure out if I can get past this or not."

Connie gave me a hug. "Just remember what you have with her. So make your decision based on that."

Ted nodded his head in agreement. "She isn't Siobhan and she isn't Bianca. She's something special. She makes you shine bright."

I pushed my chair back. "Thanks for the bed, the breakfast and the chat. But I've got a relationship to save."

I left the kitchen and grabbed my bag, not bothering to change my clothes before I left. When I got home, I was greeted by only Aoife. She swiped by me but wouldn't let me pick her up. She was mad. "Abi! Are you still here? Abi! We need to talk!" I checked my bedroom, and her bag was gone. I saw the note ripped in half on my bed. I taped it together and read it. I cursed under my breath. It was too late, and I realized how much I truly fucked up.

~ ABIGAIL ~

I collapsed on my couch when I got home, leaving my bag at the door. It had been a long flight with three transfers. But it was the quickest way back to the states I could find last minute. Worth every penny in my book. There was nothing like being home in my own apartment. Lochlan and Beatrice immediately crawled up and began sniffing me all over. They meowed in protest at me 'cheating' on them with another cat. They could smell Aoife all over my clothes. Great, two more loved ones mad at me. They quickly went to work re-scenting me.

Tess brought me a cup of tea. "Maybe it's not over. I mean you did say he tried to call you. Maybe he's ready to talk."

I sipped my tea as I shook my head. "That's great, but I'm not ready to talk to him. He treated me like—"

"Like someone who lied to him?" Tess dared to remark.

I gave her a look of death. " Who's side are you on? There are two sides to every story you know, and he wouldn't even let me tell mine!"

Tess sat down next to me, putting a fuzzy blanket over both of us. "Abi, you're my best friend and I'm on your side, really I am."

"But?" I practically spat out. I was in no mood for a lecture.

"That's it. I love you and I'm on your side. But for now, I'm going to leave you alone. Before I go, I'll run a bath for you. When you get out, there will be some warm food on the stove for you. Please, take some time to enjoy the bath. You need to relax and decompress. Then eat something and go to bed. Things will look different once you've gotten some sleep."

I just nodded. Tess got the bath ready and then brought me into the bathroom. "It's all set, so just enjoy. Food will be in the kitchen when you are ready." She gave me a long hug. "I'll call you tomorrow." Tess left and closed the door behind her.

I stripped down and slipped into the warm water. It was lavender scented. Tess had even lit some candles and put them on the edge of the tub. I relaxed in the water and let myself cry. I had made such a mess of things and had solidified it by not returning his phone calls. It was fine. I was fine. I had my students to think about and my animals at the shelter who needed me. Maybe I would add another volunteer day to my schedule. I had a life before Liam, and I would have one after.

What I really needed to do was to decide if I was going to keep my blog going. I loved *EverMorphs*. I didn't want what had happened with Liam to ruin it for me, like Ryan had with *Lost Continent*. This was different. I splashed some bath water on my face. Tonight wasn't the time to make any big decisions though.

I got out of the tub and dried off. I put on some comfy jammies and headed into the kitchen to see what Tess had left me. I laughed when I lifted the pot on the stove and saw a note. *'Gurl! You know I can't cook with what you have in your kitchen! Pizza should arrive soon. Love you! - Tess'*

I walked into the living room and made myself comfortable on my couch and turned on a movie. Lochlan and Beatrice hopped up, made a few circles and curled up next to me. One behind the other. I absentmindedly stroked both of them as I stared at the television, not really watching the movie that was on. I was brought out of my haze by the sound of my door buzzer. I got up and buzzed the delivery person in. It wasn't long before they knocked on my door with my pizza. Tess had already paid and tipped. I thanked the delivery person and took the pizza back to the living room. Pepperoni and bacon, my favorite, especially with the added bonus of a stuffed cheese crust.

I pulled at the crust, giving bits of cheese to the cats. When I finished, I put the remains in my fridge and headed to bed. Tomorrow was the last day I had all to myself before school started up again. I curled up with my favorite stuffed animal. It was a teddy bear that my older sister had given me for my fifth birthday. It wasn't as fully stuffed as it used to be and one of the eyes was missing, but it always gave me comfort. I didn't realize how exhausted I was until my head hit the pillow and my eyelids became too heavy to raise. I spent the night sleeping and dreaming of Liam. I was on one side of the cliff, and he was on the other with a great, deep chasm in between us.

~ LIAM ~

I tossed and turned the entire night until finally at three a.m, I gave up and went into the living room. Aoife followed me as I went into the kitchen to turn on the kettle. I had to be up in two hours to get ready for work anyway, so I figured I might as well get a head start. Irish breakfast tea should be the perk I needed before a morning jog. I fed Aoife and gave her an extra scoop of wet food mixed in with her dry. I could tell she was missing Abigail, almost as much as I was. There was only one thing I could think to do.

I sat on my couch and called Arlene. She was the only one I knew who could help me out of this colossal fuck up I had done. I knew it was late but I hoped she would pick up. She always picked up for me.

"Hello?" Came a groggy voice on the other end of the line.

"Leenie, I really fucked up. You're my only hope."

"What!? What did you do?" Arlene now sounded alert and wide awake.

"I need you to set up a meeting between you and me and the winning teacher of the EverMorph contest."

Arlene began to laugh. "Liam, you woke me up at 3:30 am to arrange a meeting? Have you been drinking?"

"It's Abi's school. Her drama club was the winner and I kinda exploded and said some horrible things. Mainly about her being a lying, fan fanatic and how I could never trust her again. I came to my senses once I calmed down but the damage was done and she was already gone and -"

"Woah, woah, you did what?" Arlene screeched into the phone.

I sighed. "It's a very long and very bad story. Can I skip that for now? Can you just make the meeting happen?"

"Oh hun, you really stepped in it this time. I had such high hopes for the two of you." I could hear the disappointment in her voice.

"I know! I know! Will you help me? Please?"

"Of course I will. But let me get some sleep first. We'll discuss a strategy in the morning."

I breathed a sigh of relief. "Thank you Leenie. I don't know what I'd do without you."

"And don't you forget it!" she chuckled. "Now get some sleep. I'll call you in the morning. But not until I've had my second cup of coffee."

"Thanks Leenie. I'm off for a run." I yawned as I felt my body relax a little.

"You're crazy, have a good run. Night Liam."

I headed into my bedroom to put on some jogging clothes. I sat on my bed and laughed out loud. I hated jogging, always had. But I felt it was a fitting punishment for how my week had ended and I needed a little physical pain to match my emotional pain. Thirty minutes later, my wish was granted when my left calf cramped up as I was running. I knew it was a sign my day was not going to go well. I drove up to the set and my suspicions were confirmed when I walked up to my trailer and Bianca Monroe was leaning against it with a smug little smile on her face.

I pinched the bridge of my nose as I took off my sunglasses. "Hello Bianca, why are you here?" I tried to be as cordial as I could.

"They don't let just anyone on set you know." Bianca twirled her sunglasses in her hand.

I moved past her and entered my trailer, shutting the door behind me. Bianca opened it, making herself comfortable.

"You're here early."

"And how would you know that? You've been off the show for two years now. So again I ask you, why are you here?"

"I'm here because I was given the distinct honor of being the first to tell you that I am back!"

I looked at Bianca and blinked several times. "What do you mean back?"

"I'm back on the show for the last two episodes of this season and the first half of the next season. That's all I said yes to so far." Bianca moved in and ran her hand along my chest. "We'll have to see how things go."

I grabbed Bianca's hand and pushed it away. "Things with us are going nowhere. Remember? That was your decision. Too late to take it back now."

Bianca stood up a little straighter. She was ready for the pushback. "We'll see about that. You just need to get used to me being back. Oh, and I'll be going to that school drama thing in Connecticut with you."

I was stunned. "Excuse me?" I could see in her eyes she had ulterior motives for getting back on the show. And I wanted nothing to do with them or her.

Bianca scoffed. "Did you really think it was all about getting the arts back in schools? Maybe a little, but it's a huge publicity stunt to announce me coming back to the show."

"Can you please leave? I need to get ready for my work today."

Bianca nodded. "Of course. I don't start for two more days. I just wanted to give you a couple of days to take in the idea of me being around again." She winked, gave her long jet black hair a flip, and sauntered out of my trailer.

I collapsed on the couch, and immediately called Arlene. "Leenie! Bianca! Really?!"

Arlene let out a deep sigh. She hadn't even said hello yet. She was really hoping she would get to me before Bianca did. "Sorry Liam, I was going to call you today. I could have told you last night, or rather this morning when you called, but you had more important things to worry about."

"I can handle working with her again. But her busting in on the school event? Especially with how things went down with Abi."

The familiar squeak I heard let me know that Arlene had stood up and was pacing around her desk. "NO! You don't let Bianca waylay you in any way, shape or form! You hear me? You will go to that event and you will get your woman back! Look, Abi is the best, and I do mean the best, thing that has happened to you since you got cast on

The EverMorphs. And I won't let you throw all that away. So, she's a fan, and didn't tell you. Who gives a flying fig! She isn't crazy, she's not a diva or a bitch. She's intelligent, funny, charismatic, sassy, loving, and most of all head over heels about you! Have you even read the blog that Ryan found?"

I sighed. "I have read some of it, and it's actually pretty awesome." I shook my head as I chuckled. "I'm an idiot."

"Not an idiot, just cautious, and rightly so. But Abi is the real deal. And I'm working on that meeting. It will happen."

"You're a lifesaver Leenie." I knew I could get through this with her help.

Arlene smiled. "We'll fly you in early, first class of course. The studio can foot the bill. They owe you one since they hired that witch Bianca back."

Liam laughed. "I don't know about that."

"Ha! You let me worry about it. It's my superpower."

AND THAT'S ALL I HAVE TO SAY ABOUT THAT!

ALL THINGS EVERMORPH ALL THE TIME

SEASON 4

> **Episode Highlight:** WINGS!!
> **Episode Lowlight:** Who has Flint? Spill already!!!

Greetings and Salutations, my ever faithful Everrites and Morphlings. I know it's been a minute. My humblest apologies, I had a personal glitch that overtook me for a moment, but I'm back! And wow, Wow, WOW!!!

Can we all just take a moment and relish in the joy of WINGS!! So many fabulous characters got wings!! And I have to say both Everrites and Morphlings alike should be happy with the doling out of the wings. It's pretty even and pretty spectacular on both sides. Now, although we haven't seen him in a minute, which is my next pet peeve I'll discuss shortly, I believe Flint has wings as well. Maybe someday soon we'll find out. So I want to know, who are you most excited about having wings?

Who do you wish had wings and doesn't? And most importantly do you think anyone is hiding their wings?

Okay, back to Flint! Dear sweet, kidnapped Flint. We all know someone has him. We all know that someone is BAD! However, can the bad Flint kidnapping freak please step out from behind the shadows and reveal themselves! I mean come on! The season is only twelve episodes long! There are only two left! Don't wait until the end of the twelfth episode to tell us. Sadly, I think that is EXACTLY what will happen. Grrrr!!! Any thoughts? At first, I thought it was Oberon, but I've thrown that scenario out the window. Now, I'm flirting with the idea of Zarina. But if it's her, I think she is working with someone. I just can't figure out who.

So, do you agree? Disagree? Share your theories and thoughts. I love hearing them all!

Until next time EternallyEvers OUT!!

COMMENTS:

IFollowFlint: Glad to see you back EE! You were missed! <3. Of course Flint has wings! At least that's what I believe. But where the hell is he? I like your guess of Zarina. I definitely think it's a woman.

NylaKingdom4Ever: Why doesn't the queen have wings? I mean out every fairy shouldn't she have them the most?!

IdolofIsla: Lochlan has them. Maybe they skip a generation?

~ ABIGAIL ~

I was getting back in the swing of my life. It had been a week since my trip and I was finally beginning to feel myself again. I had squashed any rumors with my students by threatening pop quizzes every week if they kept speculating. The year was beginning to wind down. The play was only three and a half weeks away. Margot was frantic with last minute assistant director duties. I was very proud of her taking on such a big responsibility. I would miss having her in my classes, but I knew NYU was lucky to be getting such a great student next fall.

My email dinged with a new message coming in. I glanced at my laptop to see if it was something I could wait until tomorrow to answer. It was never good when you got an email from the principal after five o'clock. I sighed as I replied stating that I would be in her office first thing in the morning. There was nothing more I could do until tomorrow. Closing my laptop I poured myself a glass of wine, then curled up on the couch to watch some DTV.

I was surprised to see my student Margo sitting in the principal's office when I arrived. She was clearly nervous as her knee was twitching and she was biting her thumbnail. She did that whenever she was anxious about a test question. It seemed to work for her because she was an exemplary student, and although tests were a challenge for her she always did amazingly well.

I took the seat next to her and gently pulled her thumb away from her mouth. She smiled and folded her hands in her lap. It was only another minute before principal Edwards came in with a rather large box. She placed the box on the corner of her desk and then sat down.

"Thank you for coming in before classes begin. I received this box in the mail yesterday and was really surprised when I found out our school had won a contest. A contest I wasn't even aware we had entered. Do you know anything about it, Ms. Reese?"

I shook my head. "I have no idea what you're referring to Mrs. Edwards. I'm not currently running any contests in any of my classes. And if I was entering something outside of our school district I would have informed you of the qualifications and made sure the school was fine with my class applying. You know that. That's what I've always done in the past."

She nodded. "Yes, yes I do. And that's what you've always done. I was hoping that if you couldn't shed some light on the subject that Margot might be able to".

We both turned to Margo. She had a wide smile on her face.

"We won!? We really won! I - I wasn't sure if we would. I mean, the competition had to be tough, but we really worked hard on the entry. Deep down I hoped it would pay off, and it did! Yes! This is so awesome! I can't wait to tell the others."

"Woah, woah, woah, tell the others what? Will someone please tell me what's going on here?" I was more than a little confused. I feared that what Liam had accused me of was coming to fruition.

Mrs. Edwards opened the box and slowly took out the contents. She handed me a beautifully decorated envelope. I recognized some of the stickers on the envelope. They were of my own creation. I tried to hide the lump in my throat when I saw the address. My mouth felt like sandpaper, and no matter how much I swallowed it was still like the Sahara. "Margo, what did you do?" I whispered.

Margot moved to the edge of her seat. She was giddy with excitement. "Okay, so I do feel a little guilty for what I did. And I'm sorry I didn't ask for permission. But I thought asking for forgiveness would be just as good because that would mean we won." She was talking a mile a minute.

"Just start from the beginning and go slowly please." I was trying to keep my cool until I had all the facts. But panic was slowly beginning to creep up through my body. I prayed it wouldn't come out in the form of vomit.

Margo nodded. "As the president of the drama club, I felt it was my duty." She turned to principal Edwards. "Are you going to play the video for Ms. Reese?"

Mrs. Edwards cued up something on her laptop. She turned it towards me and then hit play. What I saw was both wonderfully creative and a bit scary. This was fandom at its epicenter. A place I ran away from a long long time ago.

" Only a couple of the other drama club students helped me, those I knew I could trust. I couldn't take a chance on rumors spreading through a slip up. My best friend Amanda, the vice president of the drama club, Jonathan, Sharon, a senior in the drama club, and Tara, another club member. That's it, like I said, small group. So we took about two weeks and wrote a cute little script and acted it out. At the end, I made a speech, but you saw it."

"I will tell you one thing Ms. Reese, your students are very devoted to you." Principal Edwards let a smile slip.

I smiled. "I am just as devoted to them. Even when they go behind my back and do something outrageous like this little contest stunt." I rewound the video clip a little and hit play. Margo and Amanda were singing such a beautiful song. But I had never heard it before, yet there was something familiar about it. "The song is beautiful. Where did you find it?"

Margot blushed. "Amanda and I wrote it. It's a parody of the EverMorphs theme song."

Principal Edwards chuckled. "We have some very talented students in our midst. If only they'd use their powers for good." She raised an eyebrow. "So, after this arrived yesterday I went home and watched several episodes of The EverMorphs. I've never seen the show before so I wanted to make sure that winning a contest from the show would be appropriate for the school. With streaming services these days you never know how racy or age appropriate a show really is until you watch it."

"And you loved it right?" Margot gushed. "I think Ms. Reese likes it too, even if she'll never admit it." Margot gave me a side eye glance.

Margot had super imposed some photos of the drama club productions and playbills at the end when they were singing the song. To top it off and give them what she thought was a great advantage, she added the stickers that I had given them over the term. Just the ones that were my secret, or rather not so secret references to the show. Margot had a Cheshire grin on her face. She was clearly proud of her accomplishments.

Principal Edwards sighed as she looked at Margot with her best principal look. "I'm proud our students are taking initiative, but I really wish you had run this by me first or at the very least Ms. Reese. There are a slew of steps that now have to happen in an expedited manner if we are going to let these TV people in our school. We need permission slips for all the students involved who will be at the event. I'm sure the show will have many forms that each student will need to sign, and have their parents sign *and* have back by a certain deadline.

"But what about the drama students who aren't in the production? I'm sure they will all want to be there." Margot turned to me with a worried look in her eyes. "And our English class Ms. Reese? You know they will be upset if they can't be there. Oh! And we could sell tickets to other students who are fans of the show! Make a little extra money for the drama club."

I pursed my lips. Margot always fought for what she believed in. I just wasn't sure how much leeway to give her. I tried to push the thought of Liam in my school space for however long they would have to be here, towards the back of my head. This was something my students had worked hard for, even if it had been behind my back. I wasn't going to ruin it for them. Luckily I didn't have to.

Principal Edward shook her head. "We will keep this to all current members of the drama club and Ms. Reese's senior English class, since that is the class you're in Margot. And that is all."We are on a tight enough schedule as it is. Let's not make things more complicated than necessary."

"Mrs Edwards, since I am the advisor for the drama club I feel it's my duty to be the liaison between the show and the school. With your permission of course. I'll make sure with the help of Margot here, that all the necessary paperwork is filed and handed in way before the deadline. What is the deadline by the way?"

Principle Edwards skimmed the packet she was sent. "Two weeks."

I blanched, that wasn't a lot of time. But I squared my shoulders and nodded my head. "I'll have it all for you within seven days."

"Good, once all of that is in, the show will take over and make all the necessary arrangements with the school board. Please notify your seniors, and your drama club sooner rather than later Ms. Reese."

"I'll do it today, Mrs. Edwards. Thank you for being so understanding about the entire situation."

"Do you know who's coming from the show?" Margot was eager to know.

Principal Edwards pulled out a folder from the package.She used her reading glasses to search for the names.

"It looks like three cast members will be joining us. Liam Caffney, Lara Burnesta, and TBD. It's a surprise cast member with a special announcement of some sort."

"Maybe they will tell us the release date for the next season." Margot mused. "Or better yet a trailer for next season!"

"Hold your horses there, I seriously doubt it would be a trailer. If that was the case they would have asked for special equipment to pull that off and from what I've seen they haven't asked for anything except for some microphones." Principal Edwards shut down Margot's notions quickly.

Itried to make her feel better. "It's probably just an additional cast member they can't reveal because their appearance hasn't been confirmed by the actor yet. Let's just be happy for the two confirmed and we'll be surprised by the possibility of a third."

Margot nodded in agreement. I could tell she was trying to be on her best behavior for the time being.

Principal Edwards looked through the folder. It looks like only one television crew, BCA, has an exclusive, just one camera person and a reporter. I believe a couple of photographers from some magazines and the local newspaper will be here as well."

"Wow! I'm going to feel like I'm famous!" Margot gushed.

"Now do you wish you had auditioned?" I raised an eyebrow at Margot.

Margot shook her head. "No! It would be too much pressure. But this is going to be epic!" Margot squealed.

Principal Edwards stood. "Now, I've got another

meeting with the school board and a representative from the show. I'll have more details for you as I get them. Just make sure the students are ready. And at some point I'm sure someone from the show will want to speak to you as well Ms. Reese."

I nodded. "Of course Mrs. Edwards. I'll make myself available."

We left the office and I headed to my classroom while Margot headed to her homeroom. I quickly turned to her. "Not a word Margot. Not a word."

She gave me an enthusiastic nod. "Of course Ms. Reese. Mum's the word." She gave a little jump as she headed down the hall.

I waited until close to the end of class to share the news. Poor Margot looked like she was going to explode.

"Class, can I have your attention please. I have an announcement. Or rather Margot has an announcement. Don't you Margot?"

"Can I? Margot asked.

"Please, the floor is yours." I sat at my desk.

Margot stood. "So I'm sure you all know my love of the show The EverMorphs."

"Tell us something we don't know!" Connor laughed.

Margot gave Connor a look of death and he shut up. "As I was saying. I really enjoy the show as I know many of you do too. Anyway they had a contest. I entered the drama club and our class in it and WE WON!!"

"Shut the front door!" Andrew yelled.

"What did we win? Melissa asked.

"Everyone, quiet down. I'll take it from here Margot, thank you."

Margot took her seat. She was beaming from ear to ear.

"For our prize some members of The EverMorphs will be coming to our school to see the final dress rehearsal of our spring play and give the cast some pointers. And then take pictures."

"That's not fair! I love that show but I'm not in the drama club." Cassandra whined.

I held my hand up. "Let me finish. Since Margot is in my senior class and I'm the advisor of the drama club, our entire class is invited. It's just you guys and the drama club.

The students started squealing and talking amongst themselves. Trying to figure out when they would be coming and what they wanted to have signed. Some of the girls wanted to make salon appointments to get a mani-pedi and their hair done before the special guests made their appearance. The majority of the class were fans of the show.

As I watched the excitement from my students grow, my thoughts turned to how I would deal with Liam for the event. Even though he had reached out several times, I had ignored him. A clean break was what I wanted and more importantly needed.

It had been a long time since I had opened up like that, the pain of a break-up always seemed to take a little bit of my soul. I took a deep breath, trying to get back to concentrating on the students in front of me. I knew my mind was wandering so I got out my famous 'change it' bell and rang it.

The students immediately stopped talking and got

back to their seats. They knew the 'change it' bell meant they were about to do something out of the box and usually very creative and very fun.

"What's the twist today, Ms. Reese?"

"In honor of our EverMorph news you are going to create one mythical creature you wish was real. In fact, you have one as a pet and I want to hear all about it."

The class looked at each other. "Any mythical creature?" Margot asked.

"We have to make one up?" Andrew wanted to know.

I stood up to get my egg timer. "Absolutely! Okay, I'll give you all twenty minutes. Once we all share, we'll vote and the best one gets to decide what baked good I bring you all tomorrow."

The class reacted positively and immediately began talking to each other about what kind of mystical creature they would want or would invent. The buzzer went off and fifteen hands shot in the air, each wanting to be the first to share their creature. The rest of class flew by, and just as the results were tallied the bell rang. No one moved. They wanted to know what they would be having tomorrow.

"The winner is Connor, with his half pegasus, quarter lion, and quarter dragon pet, Nimsy. What treat would you like tomorrow for the class?"

Connor looked around the room. And they nodded. Clearly there had been a hushed conversation around the topic. "We would like your sin sticks please." Connor had the biggest grin on his face.

My students had gotten me good. I had only made sin sticks once because they were labor intensive. It was basically a shish kabob that had brownie squares, rice krispy treat squares and jumbo chocolate covered marshmallows.

Each one had different coverings and candy decorations. I put her hands in the air. "Okay, you got me, but you have to give me two days."

The class nodded in agreement as they gathered their things and headed out the door.

~ LIAM ~

I fidgeted in my seat the entire time on the plane. The last week at work was brutal. Having Bianca back on set had been traumatic to say the least. I spent most of my free time with Ted and Connie. Ted couldn't believe she was back, and Connie had suddenly not had any time to help Bianca locate new housing. I was so grateful for them.

I had stopped myself so many times from calling Abigail. I had left enough messages that she didn't return. I had even sent more flowers to the shelter but the delivery had been declined by Steve. But I wasn't ready to give up. I was about to take a big gamble and I prayed it would pay off.

Arlene reached out her hand and gave my hand a squeeze. "Relax, whatever happens happens. You've done all you can."

I nodded, taking a few deep breaths. "You're right. You're right. This should be fine. I should be fine. We should be fine." I prayed the next part of my plan would not backfire. I knew Iwould find out tomorrow morning at the meeting.

Arlene hit the button for the flight attendant. "You need a drink, and so do I."

~ ABIGAIL ~

I got home to find a package waiting for me at my door. I took it into the living room then went back to the kitchen to check on the cats' food and water. I gave them fresh water. Then opened the fridge to see what I was going to make for dinner. I had some leftovers I could reheat, but pizza sounded better so I ordered one from my favorite pizza place in town. I got fancy and added artichoke hearts, bacon and tomatoes to it this time. I poured myself a glass of red wine and went to the living room to watch some DTV. Lochlan and Beatrice took their usual spots at my side, purring as they snuggled close.

I reached for the package and opened it. It was a telescope. Small enough to sit nicely on my balcony and give me a good view of the stars. There was a note inside that read *'Some people think I'm a star. But in truth you Abi, are mine. I'm sorry, let's talk, please.'* I smiled at the note and the present. I allowed myself to believe that maybe he was ready to accept all that I was, including me being a fan. I wasn't completely ready to have 'the talk' so I just left him a simple text - *Thank You*. I would see Liam in two days. That gave me two more days to figure out what, if anything, I wanted to say to him. The door buzzer took me out of my thoughts of Liam. My dinner had arrived.

My face dropped as Tess walked in the door and Abi wasn't behind her. Tess came up to the table and sat down.

"You're an asshole, you know that right?"

I gave Tess a half-hearted smile. "Good to see you too Tess. Dare I ask if Abi is coming?"

"You can ask, but the answer is no. I'm here in her place. Anything you need to relay about the contest event I will tell her. I'll be at the event now. Technically I'll be there as her assistant. But I'll really be there to have her back just in case you do anything else assholery."

I nodded. "Assholery. Did you just make that up?"

She shrugged "Maybe."

"Maybe what?" Arlene came up behind Tess and handed me a coffee. She put a plate of delicious looking pastries on the table. Carbs always made me feel better.

"Leenie, this is Tess, Abi's best friend."

"And the sentinel at the door I presume?" I watched as

Arlene slowly looked Tess up and down, trying to hide a lusty smile that I knew all too well.

Tess looked up at Arlene, and I could have sworn I saw a sparkle in her eye. Maybe this wasn't such a bad thing, her being here. Especially if I could get her on my side.

"Can I get you some coffee or tea? Give you a chance to yell at my boy and his stupidity a little more?" Arlene smiled at Tess, but winked at me.

"Um, I didn't come here for a bashing you know." I folded my arms across my chest. I was feeling very exposed.

Tess reached over and patted my hand. "I know boo-boo. You came looking for a Hail Mary. And lucky for you I'm that Mary."

Arlene leaned down close to Tess's ear. "I'll just surprise you with a drink. Carry on." She brushed her hand over Tess's arm as she walked back up to the counter.

Tess turned to watch her go before turning back to me. "So, do you have a plan here to get Abi back or do I have to figure that out too?"

I started to relax. She was on my side. "I have a couple of ideas."

"Well you need one stellar out of this world plan to make up for your fuckery."

"Hey! I'm not the only one who did something wrong here. It takes two to tango you know! None of this would have happened if she hadn't lied!" I tried to keep my voice tempered but I was getting pissed. I hadn't come here to get belittled and blamed.

Tess raised an eyebrow. I don't know if you are aware, but Abi actually had nothing to do with the contest. One of her students went behind her back and applied without getting permission from her or the principal. So there was no treachery or malice or deception on Abi's part."

I leaned back in my chair. "Well, not about that at least."

Tess conceded. "Fair point. She should have come clean right after she knew she wanted something real with you. Right after that first dinner. Sad to say her fear got the best of her. But trauma does crazy things to people."

"Has the name calling stopped?" Arlene sat down and handed Tess a cup of something that was very very hot. I could see the steam rising off the top. "Cinnamon espresso latte with shaved chocolate on top. And just a dash of cayenne. You look like you like a little spice in your life."

The two just smiled at each other for a moment. All of a sudden I felt like I was a third wheel. I cleared my throat. "Would you two like to be alone?"

Tess handed Arlene her phone. "If you want to continue this later once we get the love birds back in sync just put your number in."

Arlene looked at me. I shrugged and smiled. "Have at it."

I watched as Arlene put her number in, and handed the phone back to Tess. She immediately dialed the number and we looked on as Arlene's phone buzzed on the table.

Tess ended the call and smiled. "Just checking. Now back to business." She put her elbows on the table, chin in her hands. "Now how do we get you back to your happily ever after?"

"I actually have a really good idea about that." Arlene took a blueberry muffin from the platter and smiled.

"Oh? Do tell!" Tess grabbed an almond croissant.

I felt like I was a third wheel again. So I grabbed a sesame bagel, put some butter on it, and quietly munched as Arlene hatched her plan, with Tess adding tidbits here and there. The two of them came up with a plan so much better than I could ever dream of. I let them work their magic to help me get back the love of my life.

Today was a new day. I headed to work early. My seniors were doing presentations on a character they had chosen to research from *The Canterbury Tales*. I was loaded with licorice, both black and red, and carrot sticks. I found giving them something to crunch before the presentations began helped to ease their tension. There was something about working the jaw.

I had also built in breaks every three students so they could grab some licorice, and walk around the room a bit. Oral presentations were anxiety inducing for a lot of my students so I tried to do little things to put them at ease. This time around I added Chamomile tea. It had helped me calm down many times so I would offer it to my students if they wanted to try some. My last measure was some lavender oil to put in my diffuser. Lavender was a known calming flower. The room would be prepared by the time my students got there.

Her students filed in and took their seats. "What's that smell?" Keith asked.

"Good morning Keith. It's lavender," I remarked.

"I like it." Keith nodded in approval.

"Okay, everyone take your seats please. Today we are going to do presentations *Hunger Games* style. Everyone's name is in this bowl." I picked up the bowl to show the class. "I'll draw a name and that's who will present first."

"Can we pick the first name?" Liam smiled as he and Lara entered the room with Principal Edwards and Arlene.

"Oh shit!" Amanda yelled.

"Language!" Principal Edwards pointed at Amanda.

"Sorry Mrs. Edwards, but it's Lochlan and Queen Ryla!"

Lara laughed. "Please call me Lara, and this is the handsome Liam. Sorry for interrupting but we wanted to meet Margot, Miss Reese, and all the rest of the class. Your letter captured our hearts and we just had to find out more about all of you."

Principal Edwards pulled me aside. "Sorry for the ambush. They just showed up this morning. They made a compelling argument. It's just for this class. And then tomorrow will go as scheduled."

"Oh, it's fine. Just look at my students. They are in heaven."

"I'll leave you to it then." Principal Edwards smiled and headed out the door.

"So, which one of you is Margot?" Liam asked as he walked around the room. He was careful not to make direct eye contact with me but I could see him watching me out of the corner of his eye.

"And who has some of those amazing stickers on hand so I can get a closer look?" Lara questioned.

Amanda's hand shot right up. "I'm not Margot but I

have the stickers. All of them are on my binder here." She handed her binder to Lara.

"I'm Margot." She tentatively stood up.

"Ah! Sweet Margot!" Liam walked up to her and gave her a big hug. "Thank you for sending the letter."

"I wanted to surprise Ms. Reese. She's my favorite teacher and I think she likes the show, even if she won't admit it."

"Is that right?" Liam looked at me and smiled. "Well, I know that we at *EverMorphs* would be honored to have a fan as wonderful and special as Ms. Reese. We heard what a wonderful teacher she is. That she is kind and wise. That she knows how to make you laugh and feel like you are the most important person in the room. She listens and is caring and gives all of herself without asking for anything in return. And most importantly she is someone you can trust without question." Liam kept eye contact with me the entire time he was speaking even though he was walking around the room. That message was for me, more than my students. I knew that.

"She's the best!" Megan yelled out. The class started clapping in agreement.

"Well, it seems there is a Queen in this realm of English learning, my son," Lara proclaimed.

"Tis true mother. And they deserve a space in the kingdom of Nyla. Wouldn't you agree?" Liam gave a royal bow before his mother the queen.

"I think it only fair to make them all honorary kinsmen of the fairy realm of Nyla. So shall it be!" Lara waved her hand up in great fanfare.

Liam excused himself from the room for a moment and came back with two very large bags filled with sweatshirts and water bottles for everyone in the class. "Please accept these humble tokens as remembrance of this day and your kinship to our realm." Liam and Lara started hanging out the sweatshirts and bottles.

Margot got hers first and looked it over very carefully. "Is this swag for next season?" She looked shocked.

Liam nodded. "We may have twisted a few arms to get this, but yes this is brand new, no one has seen it yet official *EverMorphs* merchandise for season five."

The room erupted in cheers. I tried to quiet them down, as I kept the tears brimming at the edge of my eyes at bay. It made my heart swell to see my students so happy. They were a great bunch of kids and I wanted the world for them. This was a moment I knew they would never forget. "Class, come on now. Bring it down a notch or two."

Lara clapped her hands. "Now, who wants pictures?

Everyone reached for their phones.

"Alright let's just go row by row for individual pictures and then we'll do a big group shot, sound good?" Lara suggested.

"That sounds great," I agreed. "Keith and Connor, can you help move some desks so we can have a good wall to take photos against?"

The boys quickly went to work with Lara guiding them. Liam walked over to me. He gave me a tentative smile. "Hi."

"Hi," I felt very shy all of sudden.

"It's good to see you. You look wonderful," Liam commented. "I've missed you."

I took a step back. "Thank you for the telescope, it's lovely."

"You are very welcome. How are Cassiopeia and Dipper?"

I grimaced. "They are good. I think they miss you. But you should know their names are actually Lochlan and Beatrice."

Liam laughed out loud a little louder than I think he expected. It surprised us both. "That's why they never came when I called them. I thought they just didn't like me!" Liam took a step closer to me. "Can we have dinner tonight and talk?"

I nodded. "That would be nice." I had decided this morning in the shower that I needed to talk to Liam while he was here. Really talk.

"I'll make reservations somewhere quiet."

I hesitated, but only for a moment. "No, why don't you come to my place? I'll make food or order out. But it will be an easier place to talk."

A look of relief washed over Liam's face. "That sounds great. Honestly I wanted to talk at your apartment, but I didn't want to presume anything. That's why I had suggested a quiet restaurant. Is seven o'clock alright?"

I smiled. "Sounds good." I looked around the room. "It looks like they are ready for pictures. Are you ready for them?"

"As long as you're by my side I am ready for anything." Liam gave my hand a squeeze and walked away before I could say anything else.

The school was buzzing with news of the celebrity visit for the rest of the day. My students were either walking on cloud nine or completely bummed that they weren't seniors yet and had missed the big event. I had to admit I was really happy about what Liam had done. Principal

Edwards told me about the ambush he and Lara had made with the help of Arlene and Tess. He even made a donation to the drama club to sweeten the deal. He was trying, and I appreciated it. Even if he was throwing his money and clout around just a little bit to do it.

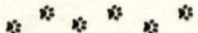

After school I had a quick meeting with my drama students so they would all know what was happening the next day. Once that was done, I headed to the grocery store to pick up a few things. Taco salads were yummy and simple. I also planned on whipping up a quick sin brownie. I was basically just taking the brownie part of one of my sin sticks. This brownie would have a layer of caramel and peanut in the middle and be topped with a toasted marshmallow topping. Baking helped me relax and I definitely needed to relax.

Baking helped me think clearly. When I was quiet with myself, and honest with myself, I knew I wanted to get back together with Liam, but I didn't want to be hurt again. Part of me, the hurt part, wanted nothing more to do with him, but the bigger part of me wanted him in my life now and forever. I had to ask myself if I was willing to risk maybe getting hurt again. But I realized I had hurt him as much as he had hurt me. No one was blameless in this.

~ ABIGAIL ~

With a clear head and a freshly showered body, I put my hair in a high ponytail and put some music on. I was pouring two glasses of wine, the same wine we had on our very first date when the door buzzer went off. I didn't even answer, just buzzed Liam in. A minute later there was a knock on my door.

I opened the door to find Liam with a bouquet of wildflowers. I closed my eyes, and inhaled deeply. They smelled like peace and tranquility. "Thank you, they are beautiful." I stepped aside and Liam came in.

"I tried to call you. I left some messages." His voice wasn't being judgmental or accusatory. He was just speaking his mind.

"I wasn't ready to talk." I handed him a glass of wine. "But I listened to every message."

Liam took a sip and smiled. "It's our wine."

I started walking towards the dining room. "Dinner is ready."

We made small talk as we ate. Much like we did on our first date. It was relaxing for both of us.

"Dessert in the living room?" I suggested.

"Let me help with the dishes." Liam stood up and cleared the table.

I took his hand in mine. "We can wash them later." I brought him into the living room and sat him on the couch. "I'll be right back." A few minutes later I came back with two big pieces of brownie with some vanilla bean ice cream on the side. I had warmed the brownie slightly so the ice cream was the perfect kind of melty.

Liam took his, and tasted it. "Mmm, this is delicious Abi." He put it down and looked at me. "Abi, I think we should—"

"Get back together," I finished his sentence.

"Really? Is that what you want? Because that's what I want. I'm so sorry I acted like an asshole. I needed time to process, and I needed a smack in the head from two very wise and very happy people. As well as a kick in the ass from someone firmly in your corner."

I laughed and nodded. I made a mental note to thank Ted and Connie, as well as Tess. I'm pretty sure she's the one who gave him a kick in the ass. I just hoped it was verbally and not physically. "And you're alright with me being a fan? I mean have you read my blog? I'm a pretty big one. And I won't give it up."

"If you don't hide your fandom from me. I will fully embrace it, because it's part of you, and I love all of you."

" I love all of you too." I put my arms around Liam as he pulled me into a kiss, bringing my body as close to him as possible. It was familiar yet somehow new territory. We were gently forced apart by a cat slinking in between us.

Liam looked down and scooped up the cat. "It's lovely to meet you again, Beatrice." That cat mewed and crawled up his chest resting in the middle. She curled into a little ball and began purring.

I laughed. "I knew she missed you."

"What do you think of the name *LovelyLochlanLocks*?"

I was puzzled. I reached for one of Liam's curls and twirled it around my fingers. So silky and soft. It felt wonderful. It felt like home. "It's an interesting name. Did you read it somewhere?"

Liam gave a devilish smile. "Nope."

"Is it someone I should be looking out for?" I kissed his neck.

Liam nodded. "Absolutely. I think he'll have some insightful comments for your blog." He moved Beatrice off of his chest.

I raised an eyebrow. "He? Really? You think it's a he?"

"I know it is." Liam leaned in and kissed me. "I also know that you really like the way he does this." Liam gave my neck a little lick and a gentle bite. It sent a delicious shiver up and down my spine.

I sighed, trying not to moan. "I can't wait to see what other surprises he has for me."

Liam winked. "Let me show you."

~ LIAM ~

"I can't believe you made me fly alone." Bianca
pouted as she got into the limousine she was
taking to the school with us.

"I can't believe you thought it would be any other way."
I snorted and rolled my eyes.

"Children, be nice," Lara admonished. "Bianca, this is
your first event since you got back. Please don't be your
usual self and suck all the joy out of today."

Bianca gave Lara a snarky smile, but kept going. "And
what's this all about?" She shoved a photo posted on Self-
Site from our school visit in Arlene's face.

Arlene pushed the phone away. "It was a private event
Liam had planned. You weren't invited."

"Clearly!" Bianca settled back in her seat. "I wouldn't
have minded some free publicity you know."

"I didn't do it for publicity. I did it to be nice. You
should try that sometime." I snapped.

Bianca opened her mouth then closed it when she saw

the look Lara was giving her. We rode the rest of the ride
in silence.

The school auditorium was buzzing with activities. A special section had been roped off for the photographers, and reporters. Another section was for the students involved in the show, as well as the English class seniors and the last section was for the three special guests. Margot looked calm but resolved as she ran around backstage making sure everyone had everything they needed. It was fifteen minutes to curtain. I just stood in the wings. This was her baby and was letting her take the lead.

Flashes went off as the actors walked into the auditorium and down the aisle, especially when they saw Bianca Monroe squeezing close to Liam. I had read all about their explosive red carpet break up. To the press it had been catnip gold. It dominated the tabloids and entertainment networks for several weeks. To see them walking in together made the press salivate with possibilities.

They headed straight to the stage, as Arlene went to the roped off section where they would be sitting to watch the show. Quickly the audience quieted themselves as they found their way to their seats and sat down.

Principal Edwards walked on from off stage right, meeting up with the actors center stage. She shook all their hands and then faced the audience. "We are honored and privileged to have stars Liam Caffney, Lara Burnesta, and Bianca Monroe from the hit television series *The EverMorphs* joining us for this special invite dress rehearsal of our drama club's production of *Merry Widows, Merry Brides,* directed by Abigail Reese and Margot Midsnow. The arts are such a vital part of the education system and moments like these help insure and remind us of what could be. Now, without further adieu, let me introduce Mr. Liam Caffney." Principal Edwards gave the microphone to Liam and then started clapping. The audience followed suit.

Liam gave a small bow. "Thank you so much for having us this evening. I know I speak for myself and my fellow castmates when I tell you we are honored and humbled to be here. I know we all got bit by the acting bug through our school arts programs, and I for one am excited to see these young people keep the spark of the arts alive." He handed the mic to Lara.

"And to that end we will be giving these wonderful students some tips and tricks of the trade after their performance today to take with them into their shows tomorrow and the next couple of weeks." She handed the mic to Bianca.

"The show received a massive amount of requests but the one written by Margot Midsnow touched all of our hearts. I'm a little late to the game and only read the letter yesterday but it truly resonated with me and I couldn't let this day pass without giving Margot a hug. Margot, can you come out here please?"

Margot came out from behind the curtain and hesitantly made her way to Bianca. Bianca put her arm around her. "Thank you for loving *The EverMorphs*, your teacher, and your school so much. In honor of you sharing it all with us, I have some news to share with you right here and right now. You are the first to know. Are you ready for the secret?" Bianca looked to the audience and then back to Margot. Margot nodded. "Come next season Mortals and Fae alike better be prepared because Kortalina is back!"

There was an audible gasp from the students backstage.

Bianca laughed. "That's right! I'll be back on *The Ever-Morphs* for season five. Who knows what kind of havoc my character will wreak."

A reporter leapt up from her seat. "Does that mean you and Liam are an item again?"

"Well." Bianca smiled as she walked over to Liam and put her hand out for him to take.

I held my breath waiting to see what he would do.

Liam grabbed the mic out of her other hand instead. "No, we are not an item. I am in a committed relationship with someone I love." Liam went off stage and grabbed my hand. I stood in place refusing to move.

"Come out with me, please. I want the world to know." Liam pulled.

"Are you sure?" I remained firmly where I stood, my heart racing. I knew eventually we would go public, but we just got back together. Things were moving so fast. But wasn't that always the way with us?

Liam squeezed my hand. "Absolutely."

I kept holding his hand as we went back out on stage. He gave me a kiss in front of everyone. Not a deep one. But a sensual enough one to know I wasn't just a friend. More flashes went off.

"I knew it!" Margot yelped triumphantly.

Liam gave Margot a wink, and then looked at Bianca and shrugged. "But I look forward to sharing the screen with Bianca again."

Bianca played it off like she meant to hand the mic to Liam all along.

Liam gave her a slight bow before turning back to the audience. "And now, I believe it's showtime! Places! Here we go!"

AND THAT'S ALL I HAVE TO SAY ABOUT THAT!

ALL THINGS EVERMORPH ALL THE TIME

SEASON 4 SEASON FINALE!!

Oh my dear sweet Everrites and Morphlings. Am I the only one completely blown away? How in the world am I supposed to last until next season?! This is what a ring of purgatory must feel like. Alright, who's going to be starting a countdown calendar with me?

Okay, I can't go on a minute longer without saying Holy Hanna. Kortalina is back!!! Yes, yes, we all knew and expected her to be back next season, BUT SHE CAME BACK THIS SEASON!!! And I must admit I need to give myself a pat on the back or at least half a pat, because I was right about Zarina and I was right about her working with someone. However, I had NO CLUE it was Kortalina she was in cahoots with. Did you? Come on, be honest!

Oh, and poor Flint, that evil Kortalina sucking his Fae essence dry. I can't wait until Lochlan rescues him and gives dear old Korti a who now and a what for! And he's sooooo close! Only a flight of stone steps away. Why? Why are they making us wait until next season for the rescue! Curse you EverMorph writers for being too damn good at your jobs! But we will have the entire break to contemplate what might befall our favorites next season. Anyone want to take a gander? Spill it, share your thoughts. And have no fear, I and this blog will not be going anywhere during the break. We have too much to unpack and too much to celebrate. For instance, who is going to Sci Con this summer? Anyone? Anyone?

Before I sign off please give a warm EverMorph welcome to LochlansLovelyLocks. I hope you feel at home and part of the family. We are all fans and friends here. Welcome!

Until next time EternallyEvers OUT!!

A MOMENT IN EVERMORPH

Lochlan pushed his way through the mirror quickly, closing it behind him so that no others from his realm could follow or hear his words. He flicked the light switch up and down, no electricity. A flash of lightning zig zagged across the sky, illuminating the room. His wings bristled at the sound. He deposited his sword and dagger on the bed and headed out of the room in search of Beatrice. He knew she should be within her dwelling at this time.

Lochlan found Beatrice shivering at the front door. She had just locked it behind her and was drenched from head to toe. A loud crack of thunder struck, making her cringe and yelp.

"Beatrice! Are you okay?" Lochlan moved to embrace her, not caring how wet she was. His winged enveloped her for a moment, cocooning her in a shield of warmth and love. A minute later his wings folded back, and she was completely dry.

Beatrices smiled as she touched her dry clothes and hair. "Thank you for that. The storm seems to be getting worse, and it just came out of nowhere. It was sunny and warm only two hours ago."

Lochlan led her to the kitchen. "Come, let's get something warm within you."

She followed without question. "There are flash floods happening everywhere. I barely made it home. My car is a few blocks back. I couldn't safely drive it any further. Wait, what are you doing here? We weren't supposed to meet up for another two days."

"I had to come. There has been a shift, and everything is changing. I fear mortal time on this plane is running out."

Beatrice searched his eyes for answers. "What is it? What happened?"

"Kortalina has returned and she has taken Flint as her prisoner. She is the one wreaking havoc on your weather here, and she is draining Flint to do it."

"How is that possible? I thought the queen had banished her several years ago."

Lochlan held his head down in despair. He had yet to find his best friend, his second in command. Flint had been missing for three weeks now. Lochlan didn't know how much longer Flint would last.

Beatrice cupped Lochlan's head in her hands and looked him in the eye. She pushed out love and comfort to him. It was like an invisible mist that enveloped him. Beatrice was special. She was more evolved than the average mortal. It was one of the things that drew Lochlan to her. One of the reasons he wanted to save her, and others like her. There was good in humanity, he saw it and so did his mother, the queen.

"You will find him. I have faith in you Lochlan, do not doubt for a moment your abilities or in Flint's determination to stay alive until you find him. He knows you are searching." She put her hand on his heart. "Feel that, and know it to be true."

Lochlan grabbed her into a passionate kiss. A forbidden kiss. They both knew he was betrothed to Isla. But their attraction kept growing. They had fought it for so long. But now with things in both realms reaching a pinnacle they could no longer deny their desire or passion for each other.

Duty, honor, and code ran through Lochlan's mind,

forcing him to pull his lips away from Beatrice. "I'm sorry, I shouldn't have done that."

Beatrice took a step back. "I understand." She went to make some tea. "What can I do to help you?"

"Keep alert. The Morphling faction is growing by the hour. More and more are crossing over into your dimension. The sentinels are doing the best they can, but still they are jumping through." Lochlan sighed, shoulders slumping. "There is another portal."

"Another portal? And you don't know where?"

Lochlan shook his head. "No, my men have been unable to locate it."

"I can help look. I just need to know what anomalies I should be searching for." Beatrice ran to get her laptop in the living room. Lochlan followed.

"Beatrice, you helping me will only put you in more danger than you are already in. I would break if something happened to you." He reached out to touch her but pulled his hand back. She didn't notice because she was concentrating on her computer.

But the shadow in the corner had noticed. She had witnessed the kiss and she was sure to report it back to Isla. But first she wanted to see what else the human and Lochlan were up to. Nyx slowed her breathing even further, her pulse slow and steady. For now she would listen and then use the portal Lochlan had referred to. She doubted the human would be smart enough to realize the unknown portal was right under her nose.

❧

F lint pushed against his restraints. The chains were finally beginning to pull away from the stone wall. He pulled as loudly as he dared, not wanting to alert the guards. He was weak but was digging deep within himself to break free. He knew Lochlan was looking for him, but he doubted he would find him here.

Kortalina had created a den of destruction between the realms. It was a new level of black magic that no one in Nyla had ever encountered. Living between the realms could drive one crazy. There were stories, legends. Flint never thought them to be true. Not until now. Fae would last longer than mortals but the danger was still very real, and very deadly. He had to escape before it was too late.

Flint was tired. Kortalina was draining his fae powers to enhance hers. She took much of his essence, yet always leaving just enough so he could rejuvenate before she drained him again. Even a fae as strong and magical as him could not last like that forever. Eventually he wouldn't be able to rejuvenate and his life force would go back to the cosmos of which it came. If that happened Nyla and most assuredly the human race were doomed.

ABOUT THE AUTHOR

Ruby Dare is a sassy New England girl. A writer of paranormal romance as well as urban fantasy and the occasional rom-com, all with one thing in common - SPICE. Ruby has lived up and down the East coast and even tried out Nevada for a couple of years. Loving the hot weather, but too far from family, she has now planted her roots in beautiful Greenville, South Carolina. That is until the romance winds whisk her somewhere new.

facebook.com/RomanceAuthorRubyDare
instagram.com/Writergurl73
tiktok.com/@authorrdare

ALSO BY RUBY DARE

Fae vs Warlock Saga

Covenant - Book 1

Chosen: Book 2

Accidental Resident - a novella

COMING SOON

The Return : Fae vs Warlock Saga Book 2.5

Apprenticing Amelia